PRAISE FOR CLAIRE L. SMITH

Claire L. Smith's *Helena* is a sharp, poignant story that is rich in lyrical language and lush imagery. The details and setting coalesce into a Victorian tale that feels like the lovechild of Emily Brontë and Mary Shelley. Readers will delight in being thrown into *Helena's* dark, poetic world with a witty protagonist and a cast of characters who are impossible not to fall in love with. Easily one of my favorite reads of 2020 — a beautiful work of modern Gothic literature that is not to be missed.

— SARA TANTLINGER, BRAM STOKER AWARD-
WINNING AUTHOR OF *THE DEVIL'S
DREAMLAND*

A hauntingly beautiful debut, *Helena* by Claire L. Smith invites readers into a Gothic tale of death, mourning, and ritual, one that is an absolute treat for those who like their coffins handmade and their tea with a touch of lavender and ghosts.

— STEPHANIE M. WYTOVICH, AUTHOR OF
*MOURNING JEWELRY* AND *SHEET MUSIC TO
MY ACOUSTIC NIGHTMARE*

A stark, gothic fairy tale for all lovers of the macabre, with language as comforting and hypnotizing as a cemetery at sundown. *Helena* is genuinely scary and will dance and haunt inside your darkest dreams.

Smith's writing is heavy with macabre imagery—lost spirits grotesque in appearance and corpses missing their innards—which was an excellent addition to a slowly unraveling murder mystery I was itching to see resolved by the final pages.

I highly recommend this book, which contains both the magic and the macabre in perfect amounts. Smith's prose is engaging and has all of the best hallmarks of the Gothic Horror genre.

# HELENA

CLAIRE L. SMITH

# CL◢SH

Copyright © 2020 by Claire L. Smith

Cover by Matthew revert

matthewrevertdesign.com

ISBN: 978-1-944866-75-4

CLASH Books

clashbooks.com

Troy, NY

"Prophet!" said I, "thing of evil!—prophet still, if bird or devil!

By that Heaven that bends above us—by that God we both adore—

Tell this soul with sorrow laden if, within the distant Aidenn,

It shall clasp a sainted maiden whom the angels name Lenore—

Clasp a rare and radiant maiden whom the angels name Lenore."

Quoth the Raven "Nevermore."

— - *THE RAVEN,* EDGAR ALLAN POE

# PROLOGUE

*Kent, 1839*

The open sky grumbled like an empty belly, the blotchy grey clouds smothering the blue behind it as Helena entered the graveyard centred in a wide, bare field. She held a pair of fresh daises in her grubworm fingers, the delicate white flowers tickling her nose as she turned into the aisle of graves. She felt like a powerful giant amongst the house-like tombstones with gardens of lush grass, white lilies and pink orchids lain before them. As she wandered further, her childhood glow faded with the last of the afternoon sun, the grounds turning a darker shade of grey as Helena turned back towards her aunt and uncle standing at the gate.

"Keep going!" her aunt called. "They're last to the left, remember!"

Helena recounted the names in her head, trying to form them in her brain as she paced down the aisle until she reached a large conjoined tombstone with two of three names she knew how to spell carved into it.

*'Henry Morrigan, 1808 – 1838'*

*'Heather Morrigan, 1816 – 1838'*

Despite her aunt and uncle's bland description of the event, all the seven-year-old could understand was that her mummy and daddy went into town one stormy day and never came back. She stood in front of the mural, waiting for any incoming feeling as her aunt and uncle's grim gazes clung to her like a heavy cape. Her lips twisted as if she were swallowing a mouthful of cold mushy peas, bottling the raging sea inside her until it spilled out from her eyes. With a swift swing of her arm, she slammed the flowers onto the grass in front of the grave. Why did they go away? Why aren't they coming back? Did she do something wrong? Did they hate her?

She pursed her lips, hunching her shoulders to hide her tears from her auntie and uncle in hopes they wouldn't come over. Tears rolled down her rosy cheeks, her chest jerking as she shook out the endless pain like a flowing waterfall.

Wiping her tears with her puffy black sleeve, Helena squeaked as a flutter of black feathers swooped past her, landing on the edge of the gravestone with its bony feet. A pair of marble black eyes watched her, its claw-like beak pointed at her as she froze in place.

"Helena!" her uncle called. "Step away, it might hurt you."

Helena kept her eyes fixated on the large black omen of death, hypnotised as it opened its beak to release a crackly 'ah'. Helena slid her foot forward, the grass sinking beneath her shoe as she lifted her arm towards it. The bird remained on the grave, its claws scraping the cool stone as it adjusted its stance.

"Helena!"

Helena jolted, her blood and muscles turning to rock before the raven's wings fanned at her face as it took off, gliding out into the field. Helena held her trembling chalk-coloured hand in front of her. A raindrop of red fell down her index finger before tumbling on the ledge of her palm. The pain emerged at her fingertip like a magic wand of sharpness, secondary to the swelling in her chest.

Helena turned to watch the bird land on the fence post, releasing another 'ah' before dipping upwards to reveal a bulky finger a few feet from the fence. It was a man in a knee-length coat, the collar of which he held to his face as if protecting himself from the light breeze. He stood hunched forward with wide shoulders and big hugging arms, black locks of hair emerging from his wide-brim top hat.

"Daddy!" Helena called, a spark of joy igniting within her as she raced towards the fence.

"Helena! What are you doing?" her uncle called, racing across the graveyard towards her.

Helena ignored them as warm air filled her lungs, her feet weightless as she crawled beneath the wiring of the fence. She beamed despite the dirt smothering her black dress before she rose to her feet, opening her arms as she were about to fly away with the strength of her joy.

The man bent his knees, bobbing down several inches before dropping his collar and extending both arms out towards her. Helena's smile faded, her feet skidding forward as she fell to a stop, her palms pressed against the prickly grass behind her. She screamed as the man's face peeked out from his hat and coat. His eyes were stark white with no pupils, his skin watery like a frog and his teeth a mouldy yellow behind a pair of grinning lips. Blood stained the right side of his face that capsized windward like a jagged cliff face, his nose bent to the left, crushing the nostril until one remained. Helena shrieked, needles

3

digging into her joints as the corpse leaned down towards her, two of his front teeth falling into the grass as he held his arms wide like the raven's wings.

"Lena," he croaked.

Helena wailed, her throat spilling from the piercing scream as she was hauled backwards. Her shoulder jerked as her arm snagged in its joint, prompting another scream before she twisted and thrust her way free, falling into the grass in a messy huddle. She shook like a trapped bunny, weeping into her knees as two shadows loomed over her.

"What are you doing?" her aunt spat.

"Daddy, he-he…"

Helena's whimpering silenced like a clap of thunder, the field as bare as the horizon. The space empty of her 'father', or even a shadow of his presence. Tears continued to carve her face, yet her lungs emptied as she gawked at the void patch of grass.

"Who?" her uncle asked before turning to his wife. "What's wrong with her?"

Helena eased herself back into the grass, hugging her knees to her chest as her little body began to shut down. Her emotions moulded together like bread dough before they seeped from her like sweat, leaving her an empty shell with numb limbs and stinging eyes.

# CHAPTER 1

*London, 1855*

*E*ven as Helena returned to the graveyard, the sun hid behind the clouds, afraid of the presence of death that poisoned the air. Stepping out from the carriage, Helena rounded the cabin to pay the driver who tipped his cap before rolling down the country road. Stepping onto the cemetery grounds, Helena racked her eyes around the city of tombstones that had expanded into the surrounding fields, teasing the rim of the black velvet gloves that coated her hands. She felt her stomach twist at the distant familiarity before she hurried herself towards the cottage wedged into the front corner of the cemetery.

Unlocking the front door, she stepped inside, the humble funeral home consisting of an entryway that branched out into the remainder of the rooms, the largest being the church-like auditorium with rows of wooden seats, an altar and a pedestal. The second consisted of a combined mortuary where she'd prepare the body and a storage room where she'd secure the chosen coffin. The third was wedged into the side of the building and served as an office mostly used for filing documents concerning the 'clients' and for discussing funerals with their grieving families.

Helena had made little changes to the décor when she inherited the business several years before, keeping her grandmother's choice of maroon red wallpaper and chocolate brown wooden panels. Although she decided to personalise her office, filling the blank wall to the left with a full bookshelf whilst painting the rest of the exposed walls a grey plum. Her large desk sat in the centre of the room, filling her with a sense of pride as she slid behind it. Her eyes landed on the photograph sitting in the corner of the desk, an elderly couple gazing at her from within the cheap wooden frame.

As she drew some files from her desk drawer, Helena kept her eyes on her once distant grandparents who only grew close to her once they discovered her strange 'gift' as they called it. Nose deep into preparations for the afternoon's funeral, Helena entered a fixated state of productivity before she was torn away by blunt tapping on her door.

Helena frowned, checking the clock beside her grandparents' portrait to confirm it is still too early for lunch let alone the funeral. Pushing herself from her desk, she opened the door to find two men standing an inch's length from the door frame, both with their hands locked behind their backs and wearing black tailored suits.

"Good morning. I'm afraid if you're here for the Wilson family, the funeral won't be commencing until three," Helena said.

The shorter man's face flashed, before a flustered smile spread across his triangular chin.

"Oh, excuse us, but we're not here for the funeral," he said. "We're looking for Mr Morrigan, is he here?"

Helena blinked, her lips dropping into a frown as her eyes narrowed towards the man.

"Of course," she sighed, pointing behind the men and out towards the graveyard. "He's right next to his wife, third row to the left, five stones down."

Their faces dropped, their thin lips curling downwards as they gawked at her.

"But if you'd like to speak to the owner, she's standing right in front of you," Helena said.

The short man remained hypnotised by his confusion, allowing for the taller to step forward, extending his large pale hand.

"Excuse the misunderstanding," he said. "My name is Mr Eric Tarter. This is my brother, Christian Tarter…we received your letter of inquiry regarding the house."

Helena eyed his hand before reaching out to take it, engulfed in her own surprise as she did. Her defence cracked as Mr Tarter shook her hand as if he were greeting a business partner or, at the very least, someone he respected. She lifted her eyes from the handshake before retracting her arms, squinting at Eric then stepping back into the office.

"Helena Morrigan," she said. "This will have to be quick, I have an appointment with another client before the funeral."

Turning her heel, she led Eric and Christian into the room, gesturing to the three chairs facing her desk. She made note that they chose the chairs furthest to each side, leaving the middle chair empty. Both men had thin pale faces with sharp noses attached to a pair of dirt-coloured eyes. Eric, the taller, slicked his hair back with a form of grease whilst Christian kept his black locks free and tussled as if he were still in elementary school. Helena easily associated them as brothers, given their asymmetric appearances and civil distain towards one another. She gave them a closed smile before sliding into her own chair, placing her hands clasped on the surface of the desk.

"So, you inherited the business from your father?" Christian asked, his joyful tone resembling a child asking about the solar system.

"My grandparents," Helena replied.

Helena smiled, the corner of her lips reaching her ears as she aimed her contradicting eyes towards Christian, her piercing gaze sinking him as he cleared his throat.

"I assume the house is still available?" she asked.

"Well, we're planning to use it as an investment property and rent it," Eric replied, bending his elbow to rest against the arm of the chair. "However, it overlooks the graveyard and, as you can imagine, it puts a lot of people off, especially those with children or…vivid imagination."

"So, I piqued your interest," Helena said.

Eric nodded before leaning forward in his seat.

"We're sure you would benefit the most from the location," Eric said. "You mentioned you live in London, the train journey out here must be tiresome."

Helena lifted her right brow, tilting her head as her brain recounted the long trip from her city flat to the country graveyard. She had eyed the house for some time. She averted her eyes from Christian as she pondered before lashing them back towards him.

"It's two bedrooms, yes?" she asked.

"Yes, we haven't lived in it since we were children, but it is in good condition," Christian said.

"I'll have to examine it before I can make a decision," Helena said. "I have an opening tomorrow."

Eric and Christian exchanged looks, not shifting a feature before their dark brown eyes landed back on her once again.

"So do I," Eric said with a slight grin. "What time suits you?"

❧

HELENA RETURNED to work with her mind fixated on the clock, the Tarter brothers' unannounced visit making her behind in preparations for her potential client. She set the contract neatly in the corner of the desk among the options and packages she offered whilst preparing to gently dab at the family's open wounds. The door vibrated once again under the weight of a knocking fist, prompting Helena to growl through her closed lips before charging across the room towards it.

"Did you forget some—" she asked, catching her assuming tongue upon discovering her visitor.

An elderly woman with grey skin and dark eyes stood before her with hunched shoulders and a handkerchief sewed into her left hand. Helena swallowed the tennis ball in her throat as the woman hid behind her white rag, her body trembling as she gawked at Helena from behind the thick coat of tears that glazed her eyes.

"Mrs Foreman?" Helena asked.

The woman nodded, her chin trembling as her bottom lip crawled into her mouth. Helena drew the door back, clasping her hands together in front of her chest.

"My condolences for your son," she said. "Please come inside."

"I-I can't even afford a coffin for him," Mrs Foreman sobbed. "He was such a good boy."

"We can take care of that," Helena said, reaching to take Mrs Foreman's hand.

The woman whimpered as Helena's smooth hand encased her cold, aged fingers, her opposite hand gripping her handkerchief as Helena guided her into the office.

WASHING her hands at the basin, Helena glanced up into the mirror that faced her, noticing the puffy bags that clung to her lower lash line. Her raven-wing hair fell down to her waist, contrasting her milky complexion and sky-blue eyes. She was noticeably thin with bony fingers, hollow cheeks and a flat chest, yet her wide hips made her appear like a pencil with a rubber band tied at the centre. Stepping away from the mirror and out of the lavatory, Helena entered her bedroom. The little furniture she owned only remained because she couldn't find a buyer for the creaky chair and table, lumpy mattress and cramped footlocker.

Helena busied herself imagining how she could make rent for the month, maybe breaking apart the footlocker and selling it as firewood when a blunt knock came from her door.

Crossing the room, Helena pulled the door open revealing a woman hidden beneath a white wide-brim hat. Helena had rarely seen her out of mourning clothes, the pale salmon pink complementing her dark skin. Her black hair was tied into a tight braid fastened to the back of her head in a thick bun. Her soft round face dropped as she peered past Helena and glanced into the almost empty apartment.

"Oh, Helena," she gasped.

"Hello, Minerva," Helena sighed, her chest tightening as she let her fellow mortician inside. "I'd ask you to sit down but…"

"You don't need to justify yourself," Minerva replied with arched eyebrows. "Have you found anything yet?""I've met with the Tarter brothers," she said.

Minerva bit her lip, glancing towards the empty wall before turning back to Helena.

"I'm not sure moving so close would be a good idea for you," Minerva said. "You can't avoid them when you're practically there all the time."

"I don't have the money," Helena sighed, dragging her palm down her face. "I know I've asked before, but are you sure there aren't any…repellents?"

Minerva raised her shoulders, her lips hanging open before she sealed them tightly.

"If there were, I'd be selling them for a hundred pounds each," she said.

Helena's eyes dropped to the floor, the little hope she held diminishing like a lone candle in the night. Minerva stepped towards Helena, placing her hand on Helena's arm.

"What about your aunt?" she asked. "Would she be able to help you in any way?"

Helena froze, her eyes dropping again, towards the rim of her skirt. She couldn't even remember her aunt's face, the decade-old memory of their last meeting squirming beneath her skin like a stitched-up wound.

"I….no," she said. "I could try and live at the funeral home, but a client might catch me and…*they* might catch me too."

Minerva bit her lips before responding, reaching to place both hands on Helena's shoulders. Helena felt an icy jolt surge through her, backing away like a frightened bunny before wrapping her arms around herself as she edged herself away from Minerva. Minerva froze, her palms open in front of her as she waited for Helena to calm down. Helena had the courage to tell her about her 'visions', but little more in fear of the last time she let her secrets fly past her desperate lips.

"This is a gift, Helena, not a curse. You can help them," Minerva said.

"I'm afraid of them," Helena replied, blunt as a butcher's knife.

"And they sense that, and they think they can take your place," Minerva replied, matching Helena's tone.

"I don't want this to hold me back too," Helena said.

"I know," Minerva sighed.

## CHAPTER 2

The house was two stories tall with a tiny attic wedged into the roof. Its brownish-grey panels were worn from centuries of wind and rain, the black roof tiles crooked with several dislodged or lying in the front garden which consisted of uneven patches of green grass and clumps of thick dirt. Eric showed little pride as he presented each room to her, the front foyer consisted of a set of stairs that led to the upper story, the door to the living room was to the right with the kitchen to the left. Beside the kitchen door stood another, only it was freshly made in comparison to the withered wood of the remainder of the house. It was also secured with a heavy bolt lock with a rag stuffed beneath the very thin gap between the door and the floor.

"Like my brother said, we haven't lived here in quite some time," Eric said, leading her upstairs. "We moved out just after my brother and I were born."

"Oh, you're twins?" Helena asked.

"I've literally never had a moment of peace," he said.

Helena followed on toe before a soft giggling emerged

from the walls, her ears perking as she glanced up to Eric as he began to climb the creaking stairs.

"That's just my sister and her friend in the drawing room," he said. "I haven't the time, so you're welcome to meet them after."

Helena shrugged, lifting the front of her skirt before she followed him upstairs. The hallway was coated in shadows with the occasional curtain of light flowing in from the surrounding bedrooms. Helena stepped inside the first. The walls were painted in a dry maroon with a large bed with lace-white covers and an oil lamp sitting on the wooden bedside table. An open window sat to the right of the room with a large wardrobe sitting in the left corner with its doors open, tickling the ceiling with its overbearing size and empty belly.

"Now, there is one thing I should mention," Eric said, clearing his throat before continuing. "My parents used this house as a kind of storage lot before they died. We've moved all their possessions into the closet in the foyer so you won't be inconvenienced but...we'd appreciate it if you didn't disturb them until we decided what to do with them."

"Of course," Helena replied, prompting a slight smile to appear on Eric's face.

"If you need storage space, there's plenty in the attic," he said. "There's a ladder by the staircase railing."

"Eric!"

The door behind them eased open, revealing a tall woman who flinched upon seeing Helena.

"Oh, I'm sorry, am I interrupting?" she said.

"Not at all," Eric replied. "This is my sister, Audrey Tarter."

Audrey stepped forward, extending her hand to take Helena's. Her face was round with soft rosy cheeks beneath her freckled hazel eyes. Her dress was plain for her upper-class stature, a neutral navy blue with loose fabric that avoided her full waist and heavy bust. Her hair was tied into a simple low ponytail that rolled down her collarbone like a river of blonde curls.

"Helena Morrigan," Helena replied, a smile forcing her way on her face.

Even though Audrey towered over Helena's five-foot-four height, she exhumed a calming presence, her genuine smile placing a blanket of security over Helena.

"Valerie and I are heading back to London now," Audrey said to Eric who nodded in acknowledgment.

As if summoned by her name, another woman, just as tall as Audrey, slipped into the room. She was stick-thin with large brown eyes and cushioned lips that spread into a smile upon acknowledging Helena and Eric. Her hair was the colour of hazelnuts, matching the freckles that peppered her pale face.

"Safe journey," Eric said, giving a lone wave to the two women before they glided from the room.

Helena smiled to herself, tilting her head away from the door and towards the shadow in the window. Her smile fell from her face, running like watered paint towards her chin as she caught sight of the feathered creature. A raven sat in the open windowsill, picking at its wings before its eye landed on her, its pin-sized pupil piercing her as it turned to aim its beak towards her.

"Miss Morrigan?"

Helena flinched, her hand clutching her thrumming heart as the raven extended its wings, sending a wave of wind to ripple through the room before taking off, growing into a blurred silhouette. Eric glanced between Helena and the window, stepping past her to close the window with a blunt snap.

Helena kept her lips sealed, the heavy anxiety blocking

her throat before Eric cleared his voice and reached into his jacket pocket to unsheathe a letter.

"My brother and I discussed an offer last night," he said, handing her the gutted envelope. "I'll leave you to ponder it, please take your time."

Helena mumbled a soft 'thank you' before Eric left the room, closing the door behind him with a confirming click. Helena waited for his footsteps to soften into silence before she released a sharp breath of relief, her head swarming with doubt as the grimness of the room sunk into her like the winter cold. In an attempt to distract herself, Helena tugged the offer out of its envelope, her eyes widening at the suggested amount. It was borderline generous whilst still remaining firmly reasonable. Helena's mind raced with possibility. She envisioned the improvements she could make to the funeral home, increase her range of services, maybe hire a staff. She forced herself to stop, the intoxicating joy extinguishing like fire in her chest as she turned back to the closed windowsill.

## CHAPTER 3

*D*esperate and borderline homeless, Helena used the last of her savings to pay the deposit on the Tarter house. Her empty pockets filled with buzzing anxiousness as she moved in with nothing but a footlocker full of clothes, carpenter tools and select heirlooms from her grandparents, lying to the Tarter siblings that more would be coming momentarily when they saw her lack of possessions.

She shivered like a mouse in a giant maze, unused to having such a large space to herself. In an attempt to ignore the graveyard down the road, Helena wandered the house with a bundle of smouldering sage in hand, wafting the fumes as she roamed each room, more so a ritual to ease her anxiety than to ward off wandering spirits. She entered the muted navy-blue living room, manoeuvring past the two blood-red velvet couches that formed a triangle in front of the black fireplace that stood on the feature wall with dry autumn leaves settled in its belly. She rounded the room twice before turning back towards the foyer, finding the front door wedged open. Holding the sage by her waist, she reached to close it, a gathering of rumbles emerging after the click of the lock.

Helena frowned, turning towards the closet door, blunt footsteps and muffled voices sounding from behind the thick door. She caught a faint whiff of coffee beans, the smell overpowering the sage as she neared the closet. She jolted backwards as the door swung towards her, revealing a tall figure from the enclosed darkness of the room behind it.

"Did you need something?" Eric asked, closing the door behind him with a swift thud.

Helena squinted, her distain turning to disgust as she was hit with the overpowering smell of Eric's cologne. He seemed to have lathered himself in it, the normally refreshing mint and other oils burning Helena's nose and tonsils, causing her to take another step backwards. The door wedged open once again, a head of black hair and pale face sliding out of the gap.

"What's the-oh," Christian said, his eyes drifting over Helena as he saw her. "Apologies, we're just cleaning out our father's things. It may take a while for…personal reasons, I'm sure you understand."

Helena tilted her head, the coffee smell returning after stepping out of Eric's cloud of cologne.

"Why do I smell coffee?" she asked.

"Oh, I made a cup in the kitchen," Christian said. "The kettle should still be hot if you'd like some yourself."

"No, thank you," she replied, her eyes darting between the two brothers before she retreated upstairs.

FOR THE REMAINDER of the afternoon, Helena sealed herself inside the mouldy white kitchen, setting her tools and materials on the large island bench before rolling up her sleeves. Using the dead man's height and width as measurement, Helena picked up the jack saw from her collection of tools that she now kept in the attic and began to gnaw at the long plank of wood. Distracting herself from the prickling burning in her arm, Helena thought back to the invisible footman who never came home from his day job working for a wealthy family in the country.

The meeting with footman's family suffocated Helena in empathy for the lowly gutter family. His employers took back the suit their son was murdered in, refusing them his final pay check let alone contributing to the funeral in any form. After carving out a snug fit for the footman, Helena reached for her hammer and box of nails, her hot breath burning her throat as she gave herself a moment's rest. Kneeling to level herself with the poised nail, she began to knock the sharpened metal pin into the wood, her attention fixated on each jab.

A soft creak merged with her consistent thumping, prompting her glance up across the table towards the door. Helena shot up to her feet, hammer still in hand as Eric slid inside, his eyes darting between her and the half assembled sculpture on the bench.

"Forgive me, I was concerned about the noise," he said. "Is that a coffin?"

"Yes," she replied.

"You double as a carpenter?" he asked, approaching the island bench to look over her work.

"Not everyone can afford a professionally-made coffin," she explained, wiping a light coat of sweat from her brow. "If they pay for the materials and a little more for my time, they can afford a box that will keep the worms away from the body."

"Innovative," he said.

Helena blinked, pursing her lips as she shifted her stance from one foot to the other.

"Thank you," she mumbled.

She watched as his eyes ran down the table, stopping at the mug-sized tin of black paint sitting by the tool box.

"Do you paint it?" he asked.

"I usually paint a small bird in the corner to help 'carry them into the afterlife'," she explained. "It usually offers some comfort to the loved ones."

Eric paused, glancing between Helena and the floor before asking, "I can't help but be curious…but, I heard that the Foreman's have hired you. I know Will Foreman's employer, so…"

Helena's pursed her lips, her numb fingers placing the hammer down before pressing both clammy palms against the wooden surface. She recalled the footman's mother, Mrs Foreman, her wilted face and swollen eyes screaming over her stuttered whispers as she began the process of arranging her son's burial.

"Yes. I don't read the papers often, so I only heard of his death after his family hired me," she replied. "You don't usually expect a murder like that to happen this far out of the city."

"Yes, poor soul," Eric sighed. "You haven't seen his injuries then?"

"No, did they publish the forensic photographs?"

"No, they described it in the article," Eric said. "I find it hard to grasp."

"I try not to think about it," Helena said, reaching for another nail and twirling it between the tips of her fingers.

"Christian and I are leaving for the day, so we won't be bothering you any further," Eric said, clearing his throat. "I'm sorry for the morose topic."

"I'm a mortician," Helena said with a slight smile, "you can get away with being morose with me."

The corner of Eric's lips twitched into a second-long smile, a slight huff of an incomplete chuckle escaping his throat before he reached for the kitchen door, sliding back into the foyer with his hand on the doorknob.

"Good night," he said, casting a deliberate smile before encasing her in the room.

## CHAPTER 4

*A*udrey's apartment smelled like sugar buns and coffee thanks to the bakery and café next door. The living room was painted a sunny beige with two giant poppy-red couches propped in the centre with soft blanket-sized cushions that could lure Helena into deep sleep. To her left sat a wall-length bookshelf that was stuffed with novels, tombs and journals with the occasional potted plant used as additional decoration. To her right, the thin shadowed hallway that led to the kitchen, lavatory and the two separate bedrooms.

Audrey and Valerie sat opposite her, sipping the tea they'd made for her before she arrived. Helena held her own cup in hand, hovering the saucer beneath it as she forced the warm liquid down her tight throat, her anxiety simmering beneath her calm expression.

"I like your gloves," Audrey said, referring to the black silk coating Helena's hands. "I didn't think I've ever seen you without them."

"They're my favourite," Helena replied, uncomfortably tugging at the rims.

Audrey smiled before taking another sip of tea, sinking back further into her seat.

"So, you're not originally from London?" Valerie asked.

"I…came here when I was seven," she said, judging where she could twist her truths. "My uncle and aunt sent me to a boarding school."

"St. Gwendolyn's?" Valerie asked.

"Oh…no," Helena replied, smiling through her pulsing stress.

"Lucky you, the headmistress was a nightmare," Valerie said.

Helena huffed a single note of laughter before her eyes travelled over the two bookshelves that coated the back wall.

"What a wonderful collection," she said.

Valerie's face lit up as if she were struck by a beam of sunlight, her clear eyes and full lips spreading into a warm smile.

"Thank you, I'm a writer myself," she said.

"How wonderful…I've never been very fluent in reading," she mumbled, glancing down as her insecurity pierced through her comfort. "I wasn't taught very well."

Valerie pushed herself from the couch, passing Audrey before judging the bookshelf, her fingers dancing over the spines before she grabbed a thick novel from amongst the wall of worded bricks.

"You can have a read of this if you like," she said, handing Helena the weighty book. "Then perhaps you could read something of mine."

"That'd be lovely," Helena said, a smile spreading like butter across her chin as a gratefulness flooded her chest.

As Valerie returned to her seat, Helena glanced down at the cover to read in large unashamed lettering 'Jane Eyre by Charlotte Brontë'.

"I've heard of this," she said.

"My father wouldn't let me read it, he said it was dangerous," Audrey sighed.

"In other words, 'thought-provoking' and 'astounding,'" Valerie replied with a lemony tone.

Audrey turned to Valerie, presenting her appreciation with a smile that filled the room with a comforting warmth before turning back to Helena.

"Oh, I've been meaning to ask," she said, leaning towards Helena. "You're a businesswoman, would you happen to know anyone searching for a receptionist or a bookkeeper, even if it's just a fill in?"

Helena almost choked on the word 'businesswoman'. It was a title she'd never heard without a hint of cynicism, sounding foreign in a respectful tone.

"I wish I could hire a receptionist, but I'm not quite in the financial position yet," she said. "Do you know how to use a typewriter?"

"Yes, I'm quite good at it actually," Audrey replied.

"I'll ask around for you, but if something comes up for me, you'll be the first on my list," Helena said, earning a smile from both Valerie and Audrey.

❧

THE NIGHT CREPT across the plains like a thunderstorm, suffocating the daylight until it bled out nectar pink across the sky. Helena read by candlelight in her office, her hand poised on a glass of wine as she hovered her index finger over the page of the large tome. Minerva sat in the seat opposite her desk, covered in a thick shawl to protect herself from the biting cold, pouring herself another glug of the wine, wafting the rich scent beneath her nose.

"I see you've done some organising," she said, glancing up at the neatly stacked bookcase. "It looks nice."

"Thank you, I took a class from you, your records are

perfect," Helena replied, flipping the page of the two-inch thick leather-bound book.

"What are you looking for?" Minerva asked.

Helena parted her lips, readying her reply as she landed on her intended page. A large watercolour drawing invaded the page with a small paragraph of text wedged into the bottom corner.

*'Black Tourmaline: a powerful protection tool to ward off negative spirits and...'*

"Peace of mind, even if it's placebo," Helena mumbled.

"If crystals get too expensive, I can recommend the occasional glass of this," Minerva replied.

Helena smiled before glancing up from the book, lifting her eyebrows in sudden curiosity.

"How are the boys?" she asked. "Hal's started school, hasn't he?"

Minerva took another sip of wine, lifting her forefinger into the air as she swallowed.

"Yes, he started last week," she said, pressing her lips against the rim of the glass. "But, um...Henry's not getting any better."

Helena bit her lip as Henry's tall figure filled her mind, a strong middle-aged man forced to bed rest to face his mortality. Her shoulder slumped as a body of guilt fell over her back, sinking into her like a cold chill.

"I'm so sorry, Min," she said. "If there's anything I can do, just ask."

Minerva smiled, reaching forward to rest her wine glass on top of the desk.

"You're a lot like your grandmother, you know?" she said with a closed smile. "And if you're looking for tourmaline, I'm pretty sure she had some jewellery made with some."

"Yes, her wedding ring, I believe," Helena replied.

"I can't decide on whether or not that's romantic," Minerva pondered with an airy tone.

Helena's reactive giggle was smothered by a blunt thud from the jolting door, disrupting the gentle peacefulness. Helena and Minerva shared a deep frown before Helena lifted herself from her desk, another two knocks calling her as she reached for the handle, her chest filling with hot air as she pulled the door open. A man in a long raincoat stood opposite her, stocky, with his eyes hidden beneath the rim of his black top hat.

"Can I help—"

"I'm Detective Inspector Harold Jude," he interrupted, removing his hat with a slight bow.

His face was round and smooth as a pancake, with a pair of beady green eyes staring down at Helena from the bridge of a thin and pointy nose. His features collaborated in a tight frown that closed in on Helena like the metal bars of a cage, her body crawling with bugs beneath her skin as Jude continued.

"You're Miss Morrigan, I presume," he said.

## CHAPTER 5

*W*ith a ring of keys in her hand, Helena led Jude towards the morgue, a heavy lump sinking into her chest as she abandoned Minerva in her office in favour of heeding Jude's lawful commands. Inserting the key into its lock, she felt Jude's eyes hover over her shoulder, sending a ripple of chills up her spine despite the warm glow of the candle he held in his hand.

"I'm sorry to interrupt your visitation," he said, his voice hard and cold as the gravestones outside. "I didn't know you offered an…integrated service."

"She's a family friend… not that it matters," Helena replied with a blunt tone.

The following silence broke with the blunt click of the lock which Helena tucked into her pocket with the key before locking her muscles to draw back the heavy door, squinting as it scraped across the floor. The dim candle in Jude's hand coated the cramped room in a fuzzy orange glow, reaching past the metal trolley before climbing up the cubic three-by-three shelving unit propped against the moss-green tile wall. She waited for Jude to pass through the frame before she pulled the door closed behind her. Bending down, she then reached into the small footlocker that sat by the trolley, retracing a small draw-string bag.

"Why haven't you seen the body yet?" Jude asked.

"I finished off another client a few days ago and I've been making arrangements with the family, so I hadn't the time, I only made sure he was properly stored," she said, tugging at the thread of the small woven bag. "Lavender?"

Jude frowned as she lifted the small baggie up towards him, maintaining his sour expression as Helena plucked a pinchful of stems for herself.

"Suit yourself," she said, wafting the flower beneath her nostrils.

Helena crossed the room, swaying around the trolley before resting her hand on the first drawer to the left of the shelf.

"He's in here," Helena said, breathing in a whiff of lavender before reaching for the handle.

"You're staying?" he asked. "Are you sure you won't faint?"

Helena's hand hovered over the bar, her face stiffening as her lips tilted downwards into a slumped frown. She turned back towards Jude who glanced back at her with an early morning fatigue, unwavered by her sharpened glare.

"I'm a mortician, is it so hard to assume that I'm well-versed in thanatology?" she asked.

"In what?" he asked, squinting at her.

"The study of death. Clearly I'm the only expert in the room," she replied, keeping her tone innocent, as intoxicating satisfaction swelled within her.

Jude's expression firmed, resembling her earlier sour scowl. He puffed his chest like a feathered rooster, extending his legs in an attempt to tower over her. Helena crossed her arms, wearing a light smile as she pushed away the regret that tickled her mind.

"May I remind you that I am an officer of the law," he said.

"Having some nerve is not a crime," she replied, passing him to step back into the hallway. "I'll be in my office, let me know when you're ready to leave so I can lock up."

With a hard push, Helena closed the screeching door on him, sighing before turning to face the office door. Her muscles spasmed, her hands flying to her chest as a yelp lodged in her throat before a wave of relief washed over her as Minerva grinned at her from across the foyer.

"A 'hello' would've been nice," she sighed with a nervous smile.

"I didn't want to disturb the brilliant detective inspector," she replied with thick sarcasm, waiting for Helena to cross the room before repeating in mocking tone, "May I remind you that I am an officer of the law."

Helena smothered her laughter with her clammy palm, ushering Minerva back into the office.

"Do you deal with the police often?" she asked.

"No, that's why I stayed behind," Minerva replied. "They're usually finished with the body by the time it makes its way to me."

"Hopefully it's not a murder victim," Helena said, prickling anxiety filling her chest as the realisation seeped into her like a disease.

"You know what to do," Minerva said with a soft smile. "And you will have to do it eventually; you can't avoid it for long."

Helena rested her chin between her thumb and forefinger, tilting her head before mumbling, "No one can."

Detective Inspector Jude stayed well into the night, forcing Minerva to leave Helena waiting at the funeral home until he finished his final observations of the body. The following morning, Helena awoke with heavy fatigue tugging at her muscles and eyelids. Disturbing the eerie silence of the hollow house, a blunt knock called to her from the front door. Dragging herself downstairs, she opened the door to find the bright Tarter brothers gawking back at her.

"Go ahead," she sighed, stepping aside to let the two men slip into the house.

"Thank you," Christian said, tucking his hand into his pocket to find the key to the neighbouring cabinet.

He seemed to fumble, chuckling nervously as he switched to the other pocket, glancing back at Eric and Helena as he continued to search his coat. Helena caught the hint, closing the front door and stepping further into the foyer.

"I'll be in the drawing room," she said.

She paused as her eyes landed on the crumpled newspaper resting under Eric's arm. In aggressive lettering across the front page read 'MURDER VICTIM CONNECTED TO GUTTED UNIVERSITY STUDENT CASE?', her eyes lingering over the words as distant curiosity crept over her.

"Are you finished with that?" she asked.

Eric glanced down at the paper and back to her before mumbling, "I'd be careful walking to and from the cemetery," then handing her the paper.

"Thank you, but I've looked after myself for a long time," she said with a tight smile.

Eric returned the smile before she turned and sealed herself inside the living room, sitting down on the stone-like couch. As she laid the paper out on her lap, she listened for the blunt click of the closing storage door, pondering it a flickering second before she set her gaze on the article.

*"...the twenty-five-year old domestic servant was found discarded in a field several miles by a passing farmer. The police have released little information about the circumstances of the young man's murder but have confirmed a possible connection to the murders of Henry Jordan and Michael Little that occurred earlier this year. The two university graduates were found in a similar state to Mr Foreman with their bodies disembowelled and abandoned behind a London pub. No witnesses have come forward for either crimes..."*

Helena stopped reading as a strange taste seeped into her mouth, her lips curling inwards as the images of the young men's diseased bodies crawled into her mind. Her body flinched before she discarded the paper on the cushion beside her and lifted herself from the couch, failing to leave the tickling concern in the room behind her.

❧

THE SHORT WALK to and from the cemetery gave Helena a cloudy peace of mind despite the itching thought of the murdered man interrupting her cleansing. The dirt road supported her feet as she walked, the fields dancing in the wind as she followed the fencing, the shadow of the house painted into the layered horizon. Reaching into the satchel slung over her shoulder, Helena pulled out Valerie's book, tugging out the bookmark before resuming where she left off. Glancing between the road and pages, Helena continued on, her pace slowing as she escaped into the narrative.

As she glanced up once again to check her route, Helena skidded to a blunt stop, her fingers clasping the cover as she gazed further down the road. A thin silhouette stood to the side of the road, a dark smear on the gloomy beauty of the greyed scenery. Keeping her open book to her chest, Helena began to gradually dip into the road before reaching the opposite side of it. She kept her chin tilted towards the book, but her eyes strained upwards towards the silhouette as she drew closer.

The figure began to shift into focus, a man clad in a black suit and polished dress shoes. His dark hair dangled like veins from a willow tree swaying in the breeze and tickling the peak of his collar as he faced the fields. At first Helena thought he was a lost scarecrow as he stood perfectly straight and still as a plank of wood in contrast to his flowing hair. Helena held her breath as she continued to advance, tucking her book back into her bag as she eventually aligned with the man. As if hit by a brick wall, she halted. Her heart clenched in her chest, her clammy hands gripped the strap of her satchel, turning her head to stare directly at the man's flat back.

"Are you all right, sir?" she asked.

Silence passed back before a crackling moan came from the man, his shoulders shifting as he began to turn towards her. Helena's stomach dropped down to her belly button, her neck collapsing inwards as she strangled the strap of her bag, holding her breath. The outline of the man's face came into view, and then the rest of him.

His ash-grey skin was thin as French pastry, peeling off to reveal his rotting skull. His eyes were coated in crimson red, rolling in their sockets as he stumbled sideways. His suit hid the remainder of his rotting figure, except for his open blood-soaked dress shirt, the tattered article of clothing like cupboard doors opening to reveal his hollow ribcage. Helena's scream lodged in her trembling throat, her jaw dropping down to the road as the man shifted towards her. She jumped backwards, a surge of electricity jolting through her body as he took another step.

"Stop!" she yelled, her hand trembling like a loose leaf clinging to a tree branch.

He did as she asked, tilting his head as Helena swallowed down, her legs trembling beneath her. She cleared her throat as she attempted to stabilise her quivering tone.

"I-I can help you, but—"

The man screamed, contracting as he reached out his skinless hand. His fingers aimed at her as he charged forward, dipping while his knees jerked forward with each step. Helena's scream scratched up her throat, her body spiking with blinding adrenaline as she sprinted up the road, ignoring the tugging impulse to glance over her shoulder. The house ahead of her seemed to creep away from her, teasing the distance until she reached the front gate, the man's scream following her up the front porch. She dug into her purse, the man stumbling along the fence line with his hands still reaching for her. Helena tripped over the toe of her shoe as she stumbled inside, falling back against the door before sinking to the floor with a blunt thud. Her chest was heaving as silence surrounded her, feeding her pulsing heart and heated blood as she reached up to force her key into the lock, twisting it to secure herself inside. Dripping with sticky sweat, Helena waited in the torturous quietness, pressing her weight against the door, still riding her fear like an ever-tumbling wave.

## CHAPTER 6

*H*elena felt like a wooden puppet when she awoke, her stick-straight back still braced against the front door and joints jarred from the tension and stress that kept her captive all night. She groaned, pushing herself up from the floor, her swollen eyes loose in their sockets and legs wobbling as they struggled against her weight. Drawing her palm down her face, she turned to face the door, tight fear wrapping around her like a heavy blanket. Pressing her ear against the thin wooden slab, she heard only the faint rustling of a slight breeze. With her clammy hand clasping the doorhandle, Helena pushed the door open, peering across her front porch, across her dried front yard, over the road and towards the patchy field on the opposite side. The empty horizon, rare pale blue sky and thick clouds did little to nurture her leach-like fear, her body hunching over as she slipped back into the house, closing the door with a confirming click.

HELENA BUSIED herself at the funeral home in an attempt to

fill her mind with work, battering away any creeping fear or consuming anxiety that floated over her with preparations for Mr Foreman's funeral. Yet, he awaited her in the mortuary, his soulless presence calling to her until her to-do list emptied.

She approached the mortuary with a lump in her throat and a lit candle, her hands trembling as she unlocked the door and slipped inside. Setting the candle on the end table by the metal trolley which she dragged across the room to align with the shelf, she reached for the only drawer in use before tugging it open with a consistent rattle. The internal tray extended outwards on top of a pair of mechanical arms, holding the body over the trolley before Helena dragged the table backwards, freeing the tray and setting the body on top of the trolley. She centred the body in the middle of the room before turning back to close the drawer.

She gazed over the human-like silhouette hidden beneath a heavy white sheet, the summits of his nose, chin, chest and feet like peaks of snow-coated mountains. She rounded the table, biting her lip as she reached down to the footlocker by the trolley's back legs. She retrieved her face mask, placing several stems of lavender inside before securing it over her nose and mouth. Sheathing her hands in a pair of thick leather gloves, Helena approached the body, taking in a hearty breath before regaining her confidence and peeling back the sheet.

William Foreman's face resembled a lump of white clay, his swollen cheeks, rounded chin and blue lips sitting on top of the mound.

"Good afternoon," she whispered.

Helena continued to draw back the sheet, keeping her eyes on Foreman's face before they lingered past his neck. Helena gasped, nearly inhaling the lavender in her mask as her back slapped against the cool tile. Foreman appeared like an uncooked raspberry pie with pastry-white skin and vibrant red innards, yet his entire chest cavity from the arch of his collar bones to the tip of his belly button was empty. His pink ribcage was missing its lungs. His heart, liver and intestines weren't there either. Helena shivered, her hands clutching her sleeves as she gazed at the body. She bit her lip, closing her eyes as her chin pressed against her neck, recollecting herself. Beneath her horror, she understood why Mrs Foreman wanted an open casket for her son. She wanted him humanised. She didn't want a lasting memory of a disembowelled corpse, she wanted her son. Discarding her gloves on the trolley next to Foreman, Helena slipped back into the foyer before making for her office to find a needle and thread, deciding that even though he'd be covered in clothing, he deserved to be whole.

"THANK YOU FOR HAVING ME," Helena said, stepping from Minerva's front porch.

"Any time," Minerva replied.

Minerva's house appeared like a thin, tall shoebox wedged amongst a shelf of similar-looking buildings. With murky red brick walls surrounding creamy white windowsills and doors that her husband, Henry, took pride in repainting every couple of years. He also kept a crowed rose garden in between their neighbour's fence and the thin pathway, filling it with Minerva's favourite white roses and blooming daisies.

Helena smiled back at Minerva as she stood in the door frame with Hal and Henry standing behind her in the corridor. Henry stood a towering six-foot-two in comparison to Helena's five-foot-four, yet he leaned his figure against the hallway wall in his sickness-induced fatigue.

His dark eyes gleamed down to her, transferring his gentle calmness through a soft smile. Hal stood before him, wearing a set of long thin limbs, with a subtle smile spreading across his round face.

"Once again, the garden looks beautiful, Henry," Helena said.

"Thank you," Henry replied, his smile hiding slight bitterness that he was too unwell to properly work on it. "Have a safe trip home."

"Good afternoon," she said.

Helena tilted to give a slight wave to Hal before he and his parents disappeared behind the door. Crossing Minerva's thin garden, she approached her rented carriage, climbing the lowered step before calling out to the coachman.

"To Miss Tarter's," she said. "Do you remember the address from last time?"

"Yes, I do," the coachman replied, waiting for Helena to slide into the cabin before thrashing the reins.

Helena jolted inside the rumbling carriage before finding stability against the glass window, resting her chin on her palm as the shoebox townhouses passed her by, all identical except for minor differences ranging from dead patches of grass to lush flower gardens, fresh paint and chipped jobs, each suiting the inward personality of their residents. As they dipped deeper into the city's heart, more carriages emerged to join them in the clogged veins of the streets. Helena began to sink into the greys, mouldy whites and muted brick reds of her surroundings, her eyes clouding over as she eased into a numb subconscious. The sudden halt of the carriage tore her from her trance, hot adrenaline causing her mind to clog.

"Here we are!" the coachman called.

Pushing aside her purse, Helena retrieved Valerie's copy of 'Jane Eyre', sliding across the cabin to reach for the door.

"I'll just be a minute," she said, jumping from the carriage before rushing towards the front door.

She slipped into the main foyer which led to the lower floor apartment via a door to Helena's left or to Audrey's flat by a flight of stairs ahead of her. Helena placed her hand on the railing, the other gripping the book as she made her way up the firm staircase. As she climbed she heard the faint murmurings of the residents above her.

"Do you need anything whilst I'm out?" one asked.

"No, I'm all right," the other replied.

Helena glanced through the prison-bar handrail as her eyes came level with the second floor, halting with her one knee in the air as she gawked up at the scene above her. As if captured in a photograph, she froze in her spot as she laid eyes on the two women. Valerie stood with her back facing her, her tall frame bending down towards Audrey. Both barely trespassed the hallway, yet through the peak between Valerie's figure and the apartment door way, Helena could see them, their rose-petal eyelids closed as their soft lips merged together, Audrey's hands rising to skim her fingertips over Valerie's face.

"Oh, sorry," she said. "I won't bother you, I'm just returning this."

She smiled through hot cheeks as she slid the book through the railing, holding it up towards them. Both women gawked at her like rabbits hoarded in the corner, their eyes aimed at her like guns loaded in defence. After a late second, Audrey stepped past Valerie, her eyes fixated on the book as she reached down to take it from Helena's grip. Straightening her posture, Audrey held the book to her chest, crossing her arms across her body as if shielding herself.

"Goodbye," she murmured.

Helena nodded, sending Valerie one last soft glance before descending down the staircase, her hand skimming the handrail before she slipped out the front door. Her hand-held firm on the door handle, keeping the door open an inch as she reconsidered leaving, her conscience pulling her back up those stairs.

"You coming, Miss!" the coachman called, snapping Helena from her inner debate.

Helena bit her lip as she glanced between the slim hallway and the carriage, releasing the door handle and listening to the door click closed. She sighed before trudging across the front garden, a heavy stew stirring in her chest as she climbed into the carriage.

CHAPTER 7

*A* soupy mist covered the graveyard, the rain slipping through like heavy bullets, the thunder of artillery rumbling above them. Helena leaned against the doorway to the funeral home, peering at the blurred silhouette of Mrs Foreman as she remained at her disembowelled son's grave. She refused to move even as the remainder of the guests retreated from the rain either to their transportation or into the home for their final respects, standing in the shadow of her grief.

"Miss Morrigan."

Twisting her neck, Helena glanced back to a dry Jude, his hands resting on his swollen belly after having helped himself to the few refreshments the Foreman's could afford to provide their guests.

"What a lovely funeral," he said.

"How good of you to attend, Mr Jude," she said, her sarcasm hidden beneath her tepid tone.

"Detective Inspector," he corrected. "What are you doing out here?"

"Keeping an eye on her," she replied, jerking her head

towards Mrs Foreman. "If she stays for too long, she could get sick."

"Maybe that's the idea," he mumbled, pausing to let his ignorance sink into Helena's prickled skin. "Either way, I have some more questions."

Helena bit her lip as her eyes rolled in their sockets, her bitter sigh hidden beneath the patter of the rain as Jude pulled out a note pad and pen. Helena kept her eyes on Mrs Foreman, crossing her arms as the simple gesture placed a heavy weight on her shoulders.

"How long have you been running the home?" he asked, his pen poised over the paper.

"Just over three years now," she replied. "My grand-mother passed away last winter."

"And your grandfather?" Jude pestered.

"A year before," she replied.

"Were you fond of him?" Jude asked.

Helena paused, her brows dipping a centimetre down-wards before she responded. "Yes. I first met him when I was fifteen. I wish I'd had more time with them both."

Helena's eyes drifted back towards Jude who'd paused, his pen pressing firmly against the paper as his thin mouth curled into a slight frown. Helena squinted, a thick shell forming around her body as she sensed Jude's disappoint-ment. His sourness evaporated from his expression as he caught something from the corner of his eye, prompting Helena to follow his vision. Eric, Christian and Audrey stood by the entrance to the auditorium, all dressed proper in black. Jude left Helena without a farewell, crossing the lengthy foyer before sinking into the Tarter sibling circle, nudging Audrey out as the weak link.

Helena's joints locked as Audrey's worn eyes fell upon her. Her jaw softened, forcing herself to make wavering eye contact, as Audrey crossed the floor towards her. Helena parted her lips, her mind wiping clean as Audrey's chin dipped downwards, her face softening as she played with her fingers.

"How are you?" she asked.

"Well," Helena replied, holding her breath before continuing with a lower tone. "Audrey, I—"

"It wasn't what it looked like," Audrey interrupted, lifting her nose as her face soured. "And quite frankly, I don't have to explain myself to you so—"

"I don't care," Helena replied, grappling. "It's none of my business…and you're right, you don't have to explain."

Audrey's face dropped, her rabbit eyes gawking at Helena as she cleared her throat before she finished speaking.

"And I'm sorry you had to worry about me."

Audrey nodded, several drops of rain falling from the brim of her hat.

"Just make sure my brothers don't find out," she mumbled, keeping her eyes firm on Helena. "That would be appreciated."

"You don't feel as if you can tell them?"

Audrey glanced over her shoulder, prompting Helena to slant sideways to see Christian and Eric still conversing with Jude.

"I don't know…Valerie told her mother before she died. Thankfully she passed before she could disown her properly," Audrey murmured. "I'm sorry, that's a horrible thing to say."

Helena smiled, tilting her head before taking a step closer towards Audrey.

"You can talk to me," she said. "I only talk with the dead, and they're the best at keeping secrets."

Audrey huffed a smothered laugh, fuelling Helena's growing smile.

"And…um," Helena said, "I've done some budgeting; I

should be able to put some money towards a receptionist in a few weeks, if you're still interested."

A burst of light pierced Audrey's face, a smile blooming on top of her chin. Her lips sealed shut as Eric and Christian hovered over Helena's shoulder, giving her friend a slight nod before she opened their circle to them.

"How's Detective Jude?" she asked her brothers.

"It's Detective Inspector now, he corrected me every time," Eric sighed, squinting beneath the rain.

"Auntie always said he was a drag," Audrey muttered.

"A miserable old man, you can see why he got along with Father," Eric replied.

"Shame on you, both of you," Christian spat, snatching away wavering attention. "That's my father too."

Christian turned on his heel, the sloshy ground screaming behind him as he stormed off between the layers of rain. Helena bit her lip as her eyes darted between the two remaining Tarter siblings. Eric sighed, catching his eyes mid-roll before tilting towards Helena.

"Excuse me, Miss Morrigan," he said. "I'll apologise to him once he's cooled down."

Helena nodded before her eyes drifted towards Jude's carriage, the driver soaking and hunched as he waited for Jude to slide into his warmed, cushioned cabin.

"Is it safe for him to ride back into town?" Audrey asked. "The road's practically mush, he could get bogged."

"Or crash, if you want to assume the worst," Eric added.

"If only," Helena muttered.

HELENA'S EYES rolled back into her blackened mind, her skull hollow and full of shadows and flashes of white rooms, blurred faces and disconnected silhouettes. Curling like a rooted worm, she tried to block out her scenery, straining to form a steel crate around herself so that no one could penetrate her denial. She screamed as strong hands clutched her limbs, stretching her out like a poised spider. Cold vulnerability surged through her body before a sharp tremor stabbed her nerves, her body bending up to the heavens. The black figures swarmed around her like leeches to flesh, the fear pulsing through her with the electricity remaining like a sickness even as the surge eased from her.

"It wasn't me!" she screamed. "It wasn't me!"

The scream passed through Helena's lips as she flung up in bed, pressing the heavy sheets to her pounding chest as she pressed her eyes into her knees. She rocked herself back and forth, her hands gripping her trembling ribs as she drowned in the flowing water of memories flooding her throat with gargling sobs. As she caught her breath, Helena lifted her face from her knees, her bedroom bathed in a deep and hollow blue. Sitting in an ocean of empty space, Helena lowered herself back on the mattress, bending her limbs to hide within her own walls. She shivered as a faint whistle passed through the room, a whimpering voice hiding beneath, calling for her help. Helena retreated underneath the covers, suffocating herself under the illusion of protection.

## CHAPTER 8

𝒫ressing her knees against the solid wooden floor, Helena dragged her personal footlocker out from beneath her bed. She felt a strange twist in her chest as she opened the trunk, the few possessions inside reminding her of the lost relatives who owned them. Inside were her mother's wedding dress, her grandmother's childhood diary, family photographs, wills and other documentation as well as the occasional small trinket from past generations. Waiting to greet her was a framed picture of her grandparents, their faces blank and soulless captured in the flash of the camera. She attempted to place smiles back upon their chins, but the years since their respective deaths began to blur her visual memory of them, their sweet voices attached to the same blank faces. Leaning sideways, Helena propped the photograph on the bedside table, tilting it towards her pillow, her lungs filling with small rocks that pinned her to her grief.

Digging deeper into the chest, she found a small navy blue box, resting her tailbone against her heels as she opened it to reveal a large ring. Plucking the silver circlet from its velvet cushion, Helena twisted it in her grip, watching as the morning light bounced off the thumb-sized black tourmaline. She smiled to herself before slipping the ring on her middle finger, the thick metal a loose fit on her gloved digit. Snapping the jewellery box closed she leaned down to place it, catching the stare of a discarded photograph nestled amongst the various inherited belongings. Helena froze, her heart jumping up into her throat as she saw the forgotten photograph of her uncle and aunt gazing back at her with empty eyes that morphed into sinister glares through her warped lense. Biting her lip, she snapped the footlocker shut before shoving it back beneath the bed. Pushing herself from the floor, Helena charged out into the hallway, attempting to run from the triggering reminder that scratched at her back.

HELENA FELT like a dirty fly hovering down the hollow, bone-coloured marble halls of the London University. The youthful men, sharp-nosed professors and other proud chaps stalked her path, their occasional judgmental stares enough to smother the confidence to ask for directions. She had yet to see a single fellow woman. Crawling up the spiral staircase to the upper floors of the grey-stone building, Helena pulled out the telegram she'd been sent, rechecking the lecture hall number and the instructions on how to navigate the maze-like campus. Reaching the third floor, she stumbled upon the first checkpoint that ensured she was on the right track.

The memorial photograph stuck greeted the mouth of the staircase, facing Helena as she approached the two faces cropped out in a sardine-can class photograph. The two men were dressed in white collar suits with long black coats, the one to the left with fair hair and slightly shorter than his dark-haired friend on the right. Beneath the framed photograph drilled into the wall was a golden plaque with bold cursive carved inside.

*'In memory of Henry Jordan (1834-1855) and Michael Little (1833-1855)'*

Leaving the two murdered men, Helena tracked down the hall until she heard a familiar voice in the distance, trailing it until she found the labelled lecture door. She pressed her palms gently against the light doors, slipping inside the stuffy lecture room like a soft breeze. Christian stood on the raised stage of the lecture in front of a range of diagrams and photographs, a burning spotlight prickling his white skin as the remainder of the room hid behind a thick curtain of darkness. In front of him sat several silhouettes of students, some bent over whilst they attacked their note pad with their pens, some slumped back to take in the information whilst some hovered in between. As Helena scanned the room, her eyes landed on a figure two rows down waving her over with a silhouetted hand. Holding her breath, Helena drifted like a ghost down the aisle, slipping into the free seat closest to him.

"Thank you for coming," Eric whispered to her. "Forgive the strange circumstances, but I promised I'd come and watch him."

Helena paused to glance up at the many diagrams pasted across the board-like wallpaper, from diagrams of various animals including horses to frogs and monkeys all drawn on separate posters with their respective body parts singled out with black lines and annotated notes. The detail Christian flung at them striking a match of interest from Helena despite his shy and hunched presentation style. As Christian turned back towards the presentation sheets, Helena leaned sideways, tilting her face to aim her voice into Eric's ear.

"So, he's a scientist?" she whispered.

"He's a bit of everything…some say perfect," Eric muttered.

Helena cleared her throat as Eric's razor-blade envy threw a stone into the cogs of their conversation. Eric cleared his throat, half admitting his mistake before shifting in his seat.

"Anyway, I require your funeral services," he said, keeping his eyes forward on Christian. "It's my aunt, we received word that she passed away a few days ago."

"My condolences," Helena replied, the broken-record phrase empty to her no matter how much empathy she held.

"Thank you," Eric replied. "The only issue is that…"

He paused twisting his head towards Helena before lightly jerking it towards Christian, his shoulder hunching as his tall frame crumbled inward.

"Our father didn't appreciate her much, so neither did *he*," he explained, his low voice almost lost beneath Christian's lecture. "I don't want him to think that Audrey and I are going behind his back, he's still quite…upset about father's passing."

Helena nodded, keeping her expression still as she caught his second-hand anxiety and discomfort.

"I understand," she said.

CHAPTER 9

Stretching her elastic limbs, Helena rose from her bed, squinting as the warm morning sun sunk into her skin. Rubbing her bloodshot eyes, she reached for the dressing gown slung over the bedframe, trying to push aside the show reel of nightmares that broke her sleep. Pushing herself from the bed, she rounded it with her bare feet slapping against the wooden floor. Her numb state shattered like a glass window as a throaty scream tore through the house, climbing up the stairs to crash against her. Gathering her skirts, she rushed towards her bedroom door, stumbling back before a thick shadow flew up the stairs. Gripping the frame, Helena screamed as she watched the black mass pinball by and froth down the hall, the occasional chin, elbow or hand protruding from the cloud to grasp at the windows and walls. Helena cowered in her bedroom, her joints jammed as the cloud circled a final lap before it flew down the stairs with a gargling roar.

Helena held her breath, waiting in the thick silence before she poked her foot out into the corridor. She slid towards the staircase before setting the ball of her foot onto the first step then easing herself down to peek into the foyer. She flinched as she saw a vague figure leaning against the front door, his palms braced against the wall with his knees bent and his chest heaving. His eyes were as wide as a beached fish, his body stiff as if he were caught in the cold.

"What happened? I heard a scream," she asked, clutching the railing.

Christian's eyes darted towards her, his pupils sharpening as he pulled himself up, tugging on the rim of his jacket.

"I-I...tripped, that's all," he muttered.

As the wave of shock washed over her, cynical suspicion grew in its place. She squinted at him as she drew the curtains of her dressing gown around her, stalking down the staircase with the tips of her bare toes dipping out from the rim of her nightgown.

"What are you doing here?" she asked.

"Sorting through the closet," he replied, gesturing towards the door with a firm wave of his hand.

Christian's annoyance vanished once he spotted her attire, his eyes darting over to the corner of the room as he cleared his throat. Helena raised her eyebrow, unashamed of her improper state as she released the edges of her dressing gown, placing her hands instead on her hips.

"I'll leave you to get changed," he said.

"Hold on," Helena said with a wintry voice, crossing her arms as she took another step towards him. "I know this is your house and that I'm just a resident, but I would appreciate it if you would alert me of your visitation or at least make your presence known once you arrive, I'm sure that's a respectful demand."

"Demand?" Christian asked, his face flashing with mild shock.

"Yes," she said with a knife-like grin. "I'm glad we understand each other."

Her bare heel squeaked against the wooden floor as she twisted back towards the staircase, bending her knees to stomp against each step as she climbed, sending Christian a final piercing glare before returning to her room.

❦

HER PROLONGED walk from her rental to the Tarter residence allowed Helena to take in the intimidation of their abode that grew from a pin-sized speck in the distance before growing into an overwhelming structure that could easily fit at least six hearty lower-class families.

She felt hesitant to consider it a house, since it matched the towering buildings of Christian's university, the grey-slat walls towering three stories above her with countless white windows staring back down towards the frog-green garden below. She passed the short corridor of hedges that led to the eight-foot-tall front door and tapped the knocker before a pale butler invited her inside.

Helena felt like a speck of dirt amongst the eggshell-coloured walls that stretched up to a hollow ceiling carved with decorative curls that worked towards the dangling glass chandelier. She continued to gawk at the spotless scenery as she sheathed her coat, hanging it on a rack beside the door.

"Oh, I'll hold on to these," she said.

Helena bit her lip as her dusty shoes slapped against the shiny marble floor, following the tight-lipped servant as he led her towards a tall set of double doors, clutching each side with his gloved hands before parting the doors with a light flourish, stepping through to the open study.

"Miss Morrigan," he announced.

Audrey and Eric sat at the opposite end of the room, behind the barrier of a large oak desk, the warmth of the wood suiting the pale-yellow wallpaper that smothered the room, peeking out from the many full bookshelves that mounted up the walls like an infection of climbing vines. The few spaces of wall spared by the shelves were filled with several gaping oil paintings, all of which were realistic windows into bristled forests and lush fields. Helena forced a smile as she made the awkward journey across the room, shaking hands with Eric and Audrey respectively before sliding into the desk chair laid out for her.

"Thank you for coming all this way," Audrey said, dipping back into her seat. "We would've sent a carriage for you, but Christian's taken it to London."

"That's fine," Helena said, allowing for a brief pause to transition them from pleasantries to business. "So... roughly how many people do you think would be attending?"

She bit the soft flesh of her inner lip as silence fell between the brother and sister, their eyes darting down to the surface of the desk. In the silence, Helena glanced over Eric and Audrey's heads to see another painting, portrait instead of landscape, imprisoning the likeness of a stern-looking man. His grey hair was slicked back to reveal his leathery skin, his dark eyes centred over the edge of his tilted nose. Despite its physical lifelessness, Helena felt trapped beneath the suited man's gaze, almost as if she were wedged beneath the weight of a boulder.

"Not many," Eric replied, keeping his eyes on the desk as he fumbled with his response. "She's one of our last remaining relatives on our mother's side...who don't enjoy our father's side either, so it's up to us to plan the funeral, since no one else is...capable."

Helena nodded, her eyes darting between their worn faces that breathed a distant grief that eased into Helena like a contagious illness, her skin growing heavier against her muscles which loosened like stretched elastic.

"Are there any special requests that I can organise for you?" she asked.

Audrey lifted her chin, her eyes hovering towards Eric turning to Helena.

"She would send us gifts and cards every year for our birthdays and Christmas, it was very nice," she mumbled. "So I'd like to bury her with our replies."

The corners of Helena's lips perked upwards at Audrey's reply, blooming warmness filling her chest.

"What a wonderful idea, Audrey," Eric said.

Eric grinned, lifting his hand from the arm of his chair to place it on top of Audrey's. Audrey smiled back at him, her face brightening as if it'd been struck by a ray of sunshine.

THE CONSULTATION CONTINUED into the afternoon, resulting in Audrey having to leave to keep an 'appointment' with Valerie. Eric and Helena remained in the study, finalising the majority of the last of the funeral arrangements. Helena consumed herself in vigorously taking notes on a provided note pad, her pen zipping against the paper until Eric interrupted her speeding train of thought.

"I heard of my brother's conduct yesterday," he said. "On his behalf, I'm very sorry."

Helena glanced up from the papers, blinking at him before replying, "You don't need to apologise for him. If he wants my forgiveness, he's more than welcome to earn it."

"Is that your father?" she asked.

Eric twisted in his seat to look up at the wall, his face drooping as he met his father's eyes.

"Yes," he said. "What do you think?"

"He seems... stoic," Helena replied, biting her lip as she weighted her chosen word.

"That's a polite way to put it," Eric mumbled, turning back towards her.

"Did you go to his funeral?" Helena asked, curiosity nudging at her brain.

"No, that's why Christian and I…" Eric sealed his lips before stumbling into another topic. "What about yours?"

The question struck Helena like a firm push, her eyes darting to the corner of the room. No one, not even her grandparents, had mentioned or asked about her parents in over a decade. Their faces had blurred to rounded figures with pale skin and dark hair, their voices wrapped to the point she'd forgotten what they truly sounded like. The only memory of them that was on the first anniversary of their death, over sixteen years ago, seeing the lost spirit of her father standing before her with his flesh rotting free of his bones.

"They died when I was six, I don't know what they were like," she replied, forcing her voice into a bland monotone. "I worry sometimes that I wouldn't had liked them; we think our parents are perfect when we're little."

"That is true," he said with a brief smile. "And my condolences."

Glancing back to the portrait, Helena's eyes drifted down to the smaller landscape painting beneath it, floating just over Eric's head. Inside the frame sat a copy of the fields outside, except under the curtain of a violent thunder storm. The purple sky swirled above the beige grass, long branches of white lightning reaching from the black clouds to touch the naked trees lining the horizon.

"Is that of the fields outside?" she asked, gesturing with a pointing finger towards the painting.

Eric twisted back around towards the wall but retracted after a moment's glance. Turning back towards her, his face grew soft with child-like nervousness.

"Yes," he said, tapping his fingers against the desk. "What do you think?"

Helena squinted, a faint smile pinching the corners of her lips.

"I like it," she replied. "It'd be nice to get some professional feedback on my coffin birds."

"I'm by no means a professional," he said, bowing his head to hide his hot cheeks.

"You are compared to me," she replied, widening her smile at the sight of his bashfulness. "I think I might have insulted a client or two by defaming their loved ones' coffins with my lousy finger paintings."

Eric's lips jerked upwards as he huffed a muffled chuckle.

"You're very good at this," he said.

"At what?" she said, her smile denting as confusion stained her amusement.

"I'm having a hard time comforting my own sister and…you just seem to know exactly what to say," he said, the warm glow fading from his face.

"She knows you care," she said with a closed grin.

Eric returned her smile, a cloud of butterflies swarming inside Helena's ribs. She cleared her throat before turning back to her note board, tapping her pen on the next topic of interest.

"Speaking of which," she said, "I can get those flowers Audrey wanted, but it might take a while, we might have to set it back a week or so."

AFTER MAKING use of the lavatory, Helena stepped towards the full basin. With a light sigh, Helena sheathed her hands free of her signature black silk gloves, discarding them on the side of the sink before examining her hands. Her fingers were wrinkled and crackling like cooked pork skin, the layer of scars coating her knuckles and palms like another pair of gloves. Pushing aside the deep twisting in her chest, she dipped her hands into the water, running them over each other. As she grew bored of watching her scar soften beneath the layer of water, she withdrew her hands from the basin, using the soft hand towel to dry them off before hiding them back beneath the silken masks.

Slipping from the lavatory, Helena headed back in the direction of the front foyer. As she reached the foyer doorway, a faint whimper reached her ears, snagging her as the following sobs passed through her. Narrowing her eyebrows, Helena turned, her eyes running up the long corridor towards the open back door leading out to the back garden. A large tree centred itself in the frame of the door like a landscape portrait. At its base stood a woman in black, a vague silhouette fitted in the distance as the sobbing continued to flow towards Helena like a soft breeze. Helena squinted as she traced down the hallway, stopping for a heartbeat at the door.

"Audrey?" she called, stepping out from the stuffy house and into the fresh outdoor cool.

The woman remained in her place, her shoulders jolting as she continued to openly weep. Helena froze as the lurching wails didn't match Audrey's sugary voice, growing into a hollow whistle as the woman began to turn towards her. Her skin was as thin and white as rice paper, her blue veins lying beneath the transparent layers like roots beneath soil. Her purple, swollen lips trembled as she continued to sob, black tears falling from her whitened eyes. Helena held her breath, her body trembling as her fear filled up like an expanding balloon.

"Where is everyone?" the woman asked between jerking sobs. "Where am I?"

"It's okay," Helena said.

Helena swallowed, keeping the bee hive in her chest contained as she slid her foot towards the woman.

"Y-you're just lost," Helena shuttered.

Helena lifted her arm out towards the woman, her arm trembling like a branch in heavy wind. Her eyes began to burn beneath the coat of tears, her body tightening in rebellion as she drew closer. She lifted her opposite arm to meet the other, her palms shivering as the woman's coldness prickled her skin.

"W-what are you doing?" the woman asked, flinching as Helena's fingers floated over her cheeks.

Spreading her fingers, Helena hovered her fingertips over the woman's eyelids before lightly pressing them against her ice-cold skin. Helena squeezed her eyes shut as strong heat flushed through her as if she'd been hit by a lash of desert wind, biting down on the plush lips before she eased back to a living temperature. Taking in a breath of courage, Helena peeked through the curtains of her eyelashes, the pressure travelling from her fingers towards her forearm. A pair of large claws latched on to the fabric of her sleeve, digging through it and into her skin. A lifting wave of relief rushed through Helena as she gaped at the raven perched on her arm. Its black eyes hovered over her, capturing her in a brief hypnotic trance. Helena drifted in the light breeze like a strip of seaweed in a gentle ocean, fatigue flowing through her before the raven opened its wings and lifted from her arm in a single push. Helena crossed her arms over her chest, curling her fingers over the rounded edge of her shoulders as the raven soared away, releasing a daunting *ah* before falling into a blurred silhouette amongst the grey clouds.

CHAPTER 10

$S$ ealing herself back in the mortuary, Helena slipped on her gloves and mask once again, taking in a dragging breath of lavender before peeling back the sheet of another empty cadaver. Unlike the youthful, smooth face of Foreman, the acclaimed scientist Dr John Howells' cold skin was creased with wrinkles and stained with freckles. Helena sighed, her breath heavy and gravelly as she continued to sheath the heavy blanket, holding her breath as she reached Dr Howell's torso. Like Foreman, Little and Jordan, he was as empty in body as in soul. The twisted fiend has left behind Dr Howell's intestines sitting at the bottom of his open chest like a fat purple worm at the base of a hollow flower pot. She didn't know why she'd suddenly become so popular with the murdered although she didn't want to compare her bad luck to theirs.

With a light solemn weight pressed into the pit of her chest, Helena reached for her needle and thread which she now kept as permanent addition in her footlocker of instruments and supplies. Wedging the sharp needle between her thumb and pointing finger, she pinched the edge of the wide slab of discarded skin that dangled into the pit of his stomach, drawing the flap towards her before dipping the blade into Dr Howell's pleather skin, watching the thread travel through the snug hole as she began to sew him back together like a gutted doll.

A soft whoosh interrupted her solitude, light spilling into the room as the door swung backwards to tap against the wall, revealing her new receptionist.

"Helena, Mrs Howell—"

Audrey froze, her eyes bulging like a beached fish as she gazed at the hollow corpse, her jaw trembling with un-birthed words before she stepped back, slamming the door with a deep thud. Recovering from her heart's straining backflip, Helena shed herself of her gloves and mask and charged after Audrey, finding her braced against the office door, one hand flat against the wall with the other clasped over her mouth.

"I should've knocked," she muttered. "I'm sorry."

"It's all right," Helena said, placing a soft hand on Audrey's shoulder. "I was always getting sick when I started my apprenticeship with my grandmother."

Audrey's throat rolled like a vertical wave, her eyes fixated on the floor as she reached around to tightly embrace herself. Helena felt a jab in the centre of her rib cage, a soupy, sour concoction swirling within as her mind darted between guilt and displaced insult. Audrey sighed before lifting her eyes towards Helena's, biting her lip.

"How can you…I mean, do you get used to it?" she asked.

"I guess, I'm just not afraid of them…most of them," Helena mumbled, her eyes dodging Audrey's. "You don't have to be, they're people but…I like to imagine that they're happy wherever they are."

"In heaven or a place like that?" Audrey asked.

"Maybe…perhaps somewhere even better," Helena replied.

Audrey nodded, a thin smile spreading across her face as she tilted away from the wall to properly face Helena.

"Dr Howell's wife sent us a telegram," she explained, resuming her original enquiry. "She would like to move up the funeral to Wednesday. She'll be popping in tomorrow. I'll make sure she's seen."

"Thank you, Audrey," Helena replied, a slight warmth invading the cold centre of her chest.

A HEAVY BLUE blanket fell over the empty countryside, the flat plains and distant mansions but shadows beneath the beaming gaze of the soapy moon. Slipping into her white flowing, woolen nightgown, Helena began to pack away the remainder of her freshly washed clothes into the large wardrobe, hanging them like dead criminals on display. Closing the heavy doors, she turned towards the bed, drawing her raven-wing hair over her shoulder before braiding it. As she reached the desired left side of the bed, she tied off her finished plait and pressed her open palms against the mattress as she lowered herself into its stiff embrace.

Amongst the creaking of the bed frame emerged a low groan, throat-born and rumbling like a beast's growl. Helena sat up in bed, staring out the open doorframe and into the moonlight-dipped hallway that breathed tightening tension back into the bedroom. Swallowing the lump in her throat, Helena set her bare feet back against the cool wooden floor, shaking the sinister thoughts from her mind as she crossed the darkened room.

She reached for the doorhandle, clasping the rounded edge in her palm before she edged it forward. Another loud shriek halted her, the railing of the stairwell across from her creaking as a pair of blackened hands reached to clasp the prison-bar railing, the rotting fingers clenching as it pulled itself up. A bald head emerged from the gap between floors, red patches of flesh and blood glistening against the moonlight. Helena lost her breath as a pair of devil red eyes glared at her, the marble-sized pupils striking her, pulling her into a prison of reeling numbness.

"Come here!" it growled.

With cold sweat peppering her forehead and stroking her back, Helena forced her jarred body to move. Slamming the door, she braced herself against it, her fumbling hands clasping the key as its chants and throaty growls called to her from the other side. After tugging at the knob to test the lock's strength, Helena fled like a frightened dove to her bed, burying herself beneath the covers, trembling as her inner child screamed wishing for the covers to turn into a pair of comforting arms to rock her into calmness.

# CHAPTER 11

*A*fter fixing herself a cup of cheap tea, Helena carried her warm mug from the kitchen, crossing the foyer to begin her assent up the stairs. She heard faint rustling from the foyer storage cupboard, a brief thought passing through her head regarding the Tarter brothers before she resumed her climb. With one hand on the railing and the other clutching the cup, the liquid inside wobbling like an encased ocean, Helena reached the peak of the staircase. She began to lift the cup to her lips, the stream prickling her nose before a low wail echoed through the house. Helena froze, a splash of hot tea running down the silk of her gloves, burning her wrist as she lowered the cup from her lips. Squealing behind sealed lips, she set it down on the surface of the railing, her heart still pulsing from the fright.

"Mr Tarter!" she called, hoping either would answer her.

Helena waited as thick silence filled the space. Placing her hand over her chest, she began to pace back towards the staircase before staring down the thin tunnel of steps.

"We're all right!" Eric called. "A box just fell on Christian's head!"

"Shut it, Eric!"

Helena chuckled, rolling her eyes before she turned to pick up her cup, resuming the stroll to her bedroom. And yet a cold chill crawled up her spine, her shoulders hunching as sudden caution tickled her back. As she pulled open her door, she began to twist around to address the itch, her teacup slipping from her numb grip and shattering on the floor. Helena's breath wedged in her throat as she watched him climb on top of the railing, his bone-like arms wobbling as he slung himself over, an animalistic moan easing from his rotting lips as he gazed at her. The ceramic of the cup crunched beneath Helena's shoes as she eased her foot backwards, her eyes running across his ink-black skin, rotting pink flesh and clouded eyes with the signature red pupils.

Her jaw trembled and her body clenched as she whispered, "Who are you?"

He stood frozen in place, the death easing off him like a strong cologne, the smell feeding Helena's internal dread. Like a moth flying towards a light, he soared towards her, his hand latching on to her shoulder, his palm pressing against her exposed collarbone. The flesh beneath her skin froze, her whole body streaming with an icy cold that locked her in place. Helena's jaw dropped as the half-forgotten feeling returned, her throat squeezing as she stared directly into his burning red eyes. Then came the heat, pulsing his palm like a hot coal and sinking into her skin. The burning pain awakened Helena, tearing her from her fear-induced prison as she released a piercing scream.

Twisting from his grip, Helena sprinted into her bedroom, her eyes darting from wall to wall until they landed on the giant wardrobe. His fingers tickled the surface of her back as she dove inside, slamming the doors shut behind her. Helena pulled her knees to her chest, her cheek resting against the back of the cupboard, hip nudged against the door, back and toes cramped into either corner of the space. She squeezed her eyes shut as the cabin shook, jolting left and right. The door trembled, a hollow scream calling to her behind the thick wooden doors.

Helena dug her gloved fingers into her hair, pressing as the cupboard began to settle, rattling like a dropped coin until gradually easing to a stop. A deep growl continued to send a wave of sharp chills down her spine before it too eased into thin silence.

Helena's fear breathed from her as time passed, shimmering down to pulsing anxiety that prickled her skin like an insect's ticklish legs. Taking in a deep breath, Helena pressed her hand against the wardrobe door, a new wave of cold dread filling her as it did not bend to her force. She tried again, pressing against the doors as it continued to buckle under her weight, the bronze handles taunting her from the opposite side.

Her body began to lock up, curling inwards as she eased onto the floor of the wardrobe.

Gripping her ankles, she began to tremble like a frightened rabbit. Her panting morphed into whistling whimpers as the darkened wood faded into mouldy-white tiles crawling along the floor and up the walls that crept inwards as several screams sliced Helena's throat. Her body curled deeper into itself, her nose pressing between her knees as she recoiled from the cold hands that reached towards her from the dark. The stick of light peeking in from the thin space between the double doors began to close as if trapping her forever inside.

A sudden burst of light cast over her like a white blanket, her body reaching towards it as she fell from the wardrobe, hitting the bedroom floor with a hard thud. The fresh air sunk into her skin, yet she continued to tremble, tears streaming down her cheeks as she gawked at the pair of polished dress shoes pointing towards her. Her eyes darted up at a pair of long legs, a torso and a face that morphed from familiar into a darkened silhouette as a heavy black hid its features, a mouldy grey filling the walls to complete her delusion.

"Are you all right?" the figure asked.

"Don't touch me!" Helena screamed, slamming the wardrobe doors with her back as she kicked her heels against the floor.

Eric retracted his hands, attaching his knuckles to his chest with his palms facing towards her. Helena rode out her panic, sinking back into reality as her tight muscles limpened and body lightened like a floating corpse. Her relief was quickly replaced as a rock sunk from her chest into the pit of her stomach, looking back up at a wide-eyed Eric.

"I'm sorry, I—"

"Don't be," he interrupted, tilting his head. "Claustrophobia?"

Helena bit her lip, hiding her face in her clammy hands.

"Yes…I just got overwhelmed," she mumbled.

Eric nodded, watching as she gripped the wardrobe door handle, drawing herself to her feet before adjusting her white blouse with awkward tugs.

"I'll get you some water," Eric said, backtracking towards the door.

"Thank you," she replied.

Helena bit back her bitterness, a lump lifting into her throat as she stared down at Detective Jude. He'd led himself into her living room after slipping by her at the door, propping himself upon one of the red velvet couches like a stray cat, nodding to the space beside him.

"I just have a few more questions," he said with a smile.

Helena's eyes narrowed as she took a step towards him, teasing her comfort zone, she sat down beside him, facing the fireplace in front of her rather than tilting towards him.

"What is it even about?" she said. "I'd be able to help more if I knew."

Jude didn't answer, reaching across the space between them to grasp her hand, drawing it towards him to encase it in both of his own. Helena held her breath, gawking back at his wide sickly-sweet grin as her hand cooked in the oven of his palms. Despite the insects crawling beneath her skin, she was grateful that she was wearing her gloves, reducing her already crawling discomfort.

"First, I wanted to express my condolences for your grandparents," he said.

"Thank you," she replied, her tone as edged as her stare. "Although, you're quite late, they had both been deceased for several years now."

"Oh yes, forgive me," he replied, lifting his lips to reveal his teeth as he glanced around the living room. "Have you lived here long?"

"Two months now," she replied.

"The area is lovely despite the unfortunate circumstances of Mr Foreman's murder," he said, leaving a thick pause between them before counting. "I understand you came into your grandparents' care when you were fifteen years old, yes?"

"Yes," she replied.

"And...before then?"

"I lived with my aunt and uncle."

"Yes, but in between then?"

Helena felt the lump in her throat swell, a light layer of

sweat coating her back as her blood thickened in her quivering veins.

"If I recall your file correctly, you had a lengthy eight year stay at St. Orcus," Jude said, his high-pitched tone sending chills down Helena's body.

Helena attempted to retract her hand, her arm snagging as Jude tightened his grip, his hands clutching hers, their interlock trembling as she tried to pull away. Jude's grin faded away, his face turning into stone as he stared at her with noncommittal coldness. Helena swallowed, her chest trembling as she forced a reply.

"Yes, and I was released," she said, her tone as fragile as light rain. "A child suffers when their parents die."

"As well as losing an uncle, I imagine," Jude replied. "They never caught the assailant, did they?"

Helena didn't reply, trapped beneath Jude's heavy gaze as she hunched over, her shoulders dropping and spine curling forward. Jude's eyes lowered down to their hands, moving his fingers to reveal her black ring that she'd worn religiously since stumbling upon it.

"What a pretty ring," he said, smile returning to his face.

"I-it's meant to repel bad omens," Helena stuttered.

"You believe in witchcraft, Miss Morrigan?" Jude said, glancing back up towards her.

Helena flinched, biting her lip as her mind searched for the perfect response amidst her beehive brain. As she opened her jaw, a blunt knock came from the foyer followed by a barking voice.

"Miss Morrigan!"

"Excuse me," she said, pushing herself from the couch.

Picking up her skirts, Helena sped towards the foyer door, pushing the door open like a bird's wings lifting. Latching the front door handle, she drew back to reveal Eric drenched, dressed in a long raincoat. In his hands was a thick white card that he had been fumbling with to occupy himself as he waited for her in the mild rain.

"I'm sorry to intrude but I," he began before pausing, "oh, Detective Jude."

Helena glanced over her shoulder to find Jude standing in the centre of the foyer, his hands tied behind his back as he puffed his chest. She stepped back to allow Eric to walk through, removing his hat as pebbles of rain fell from him and onto the wooden floor panels.

"I have a guest, I believe it's time to go," she said to Jude.

"It's his house," Jude said, jerking his head towards Eric.

"It's my space," she replied, firming her voice.

Jude's slimy eyes glanced over towards Eric, calling for support until Eric shattered that assumption.

"You heard her," Eric said, brushing his head clean of water with a few flicks of his fingers.

Jude's face dropped, frozen in brief shock before a wet grin spread on his face as he headed towards the open front door with a prolonged stride, pausing as he aligned with Eric.

"You're not at all like your father," he said, keeping his smile. "He was a smart man, just like your brother."

Eric's face soured, lines creasing his normally soft face as he stepped towards Jude, his dark eyes fixated on the grinning official.

"He was smart enough to not rely on others to survive," he replied, "if he taught me anything."

Jude's smile fell, the corners of his lips denting his chin before he returned to a wintry glare. Helena tightened her grip on the door, holding her breath as she squinted beneath Jude's light scowl, tilting her head to gesture him out the door.

"Miss Morrigan," he acknowledged before stepping out the house.

Helena sighed as she pushed the door shut, curling her

lips inwards as she turned towards Eric who cleared his throat, tucking his top hat under his arm to reveal the white card still in his grip.

"Anyway, I was on my way home, Audrey wanted me to give this to you," he said.

Helena stepped toward him, opening the folded card to quickly scan the neat cursive writing.

*'Dear Helena,*

*I hope this finds you well. I hope you would accept this invitation to attend dinner with Valerie and I this Sunday evening. We have reservations at...'*

"Thank you," she said, folding the card to finish later.

Eric smiled, a warm contrast to the glare he'd presented to Jude, pressing his hat back on his head before squinting towards the door.

"He should be gone by now, good afternoon," he said.

"If he isn't, I wish you luck," Helena replied.

Eric huffed a single chuckle before he reached for the door, slipping behind it with a lasting grin. The left corner of Helena's lips pierced her cheek, releasing a lazy 'hm' before returning to the living room.

## CHAPTER 12

*H*elena carried prickling concern as she stepped into Minerva's consultation room, a smile placed across her face so as to not worry her friend. The study was larger than Helena's with a warm beige paintjob and a red circular rug holding a spacious desk and two hugging armchairs.

"Would you like to sit down?" Minerva asked.

"Um, no, there's something I have to show you," she said.

Helena reached up to unbutton her jacket, slinging the fabric over one of the armchairs before hooking her neckline in the bend of her finger then dragging downwards, the reveal causing Minerva's hand to fly over her gaping lips.

"God, Helena," Minerva gasped.

The burn matched the ones on her hands although flaming red and still prickling her skin. It travelled from the peak of her shoulder and spread down to the swell of her breast, the sight leaving Minerva with a steep frown.

"The last time I'd seen that happen," Helena said, tugging at the rim of her gloves, "was with my uncle."

"Yes, that happens when they try to take your place," Minerva said, her voice thin from shock.

"Yes, but…he just grabbed me," Helena explained.

Minerva glanced up to Helena, her eyes darting between her face and the burn before asking.

"For how long?"

"A few seconds, he didn't have time to try," she replied.

Minerva sighed, releasing Helena's blouse as she straightened her spine, her lips hanging open as she sighed.

"I…don't know, Helena."

"I won't try to help, it's too dangerous."

"I don't think that one wants to be helped," Minerva said. "Are you sure that you're safe there?"

Helena bit her lip as she adjusted her shirt, deep regret poisoning her chest as she lowered her eyes towards the floor.

"I spent my last savings on the deposit," she said. "It's the Tarter house or the streets."

HELENA HADN'T stepped foot inside a restaurant since she was five, the same childhood wonder lingering within her as she slid into her seat across from Valerie and Audrey. The table was coated in a deep red veil with a four-finger candle holder standing in the centre, surrounded by a circlet of white roses.

Wooden panels ran up the tall walls, stopping three-quarters of the wall to frame a woodland scenery that climbed to the ceiling and continued around the room. Large chandeliers hung from the roof, dangling from strong chains with circular rows of gleaming candles whose warm glow filled the bustling room lined with identical red tables with gaping space for dancing in the centre.

Behind them sat a quartet of strings that hummed a drifting tune that could easily fill any uncomfortable silence.

She snapped out of her awestruck gaze to turn back towards Audrey and Valerie who had also settled comfortably in their seats.

"How far along are you?" Audrey asked Valerie.

"I should be finished with the first draft in a couple of weeks," she replied.

"When will you finally let me read it?" Audrey asked with a wide grin.

"When it's ready to be read," Valerie chirped.

Their conversion leaked off them and sunk into Helena across the table, her being filling with glowing warmth that forced a smile on her face. It remained as the waiter arrived with a trio of menus, presenting each to them with a gentle flourish. Helena kept her eyes off the prices as to not smother her appetite. Helena hadn't the finances to feed herself so well in a long time, slight guilt slipping into her chest as she remembered that her friends were paying for her meal.

"Helena," Audrey said, prompting her to lift her eyes from the menu, "thank you again for coming, I know it was such short notice."

Helena smiled back at Audrey before turning back to the menu, still ordering the cheapest options she could find. She allowed herself to slip into the conversation and the contagious joy it brought, forgetting briefly about her financial hardships and the deep burns that she hid under her modest dress. Even as the food arrived, the rich and soothing tastes couldn't compare to the glow her company gave her.

As she lifted her eyes from the now empty plate, Helena's engulfing delight evaporated as she saw Audrey glancing off into the distance, almost sullen by the scene before her. Helena tilted her head to gaze over the centre of the room, a solemn weight drifted from Audrey and on to her like a faint sickness.

A large party seated to the back of the room had brought themselves into the centre of the ballroom for a dance, commencing with the band to create a synchronised circle of physical patterns. Helena bit her lip as she glanced between Audrey and Valerie, the sympathy and unspoken bitterness staining the air around them.

"I'm going to the lavatory," Valerie said, lifting herself from her seat.

"I'll come with you," Helena said.

Pushing her chair back beneath the table, Helena sent Audrey a bright smile before following Valerie into the conjoined casino. Similar to the dining room, the casino was bustling with loud voices and heavy bodies, except each and every one of them clung to gambling tables. Like vultures swarming a dead carcass, they played, their expressions ranging from intense gawks, defeated frowns and aroused grins. Helena glued herself to Valerie as they slid through the crowd, their hands interlocked as to not lose each other. As they reached an opening in the centre of the room, Helena sighed as she felt the comfort of open space, the comfort easing from her as her eyes landed on a familiar face.

Helena froze in her place as Jude lifted his vision towards her, placing his palms flat on the poker table as he squinted back at her with pursed lips. Helena straightened her spine despite the anxiety that pressed down on her shoulders, hardening her expression to combat his.

"What is it?" Valerie asked, tugging on Helena's hand.

Valerie stepped towards Helena and into Jude's field of vision, flinching once she fell under his softened scowl.

"Come on," she whispered.

Helena let Valerie pull her back into the crowd, her eyes

lingering over Jude as he turned back to the gambling table, his scowl increasing as he read his row of cards.

"I'm not surprised he'd be back at that table," Valerie sighed. "He's in horrible debt apparently, that's why you never see him change clothes."

"If he weren't so horrid, I'd feel sorry for the rude little…" Helena muttered, pausing as a thought pushed its way to the front of her mind. "Audrey knows him, doesn't she?"

"He was friends with her father," Valerie replied, pursing her plump lips.

A shadow sprouted across Valerie's face, darkness growing beneath her usually sunny glow.

"Oh, I haven't heard much good concerning the late Mr Tarter," Helena replied, "if you don't mind me saying."

"First time I met Audrey, she was crying in a hallway, I don't know what he did to her but," Valerie said, her voice as blunt as a caveman's spear, "if I could go back in time, I would've hung him."

"Setting him on fire would hurt more," Helena replied with a grin.

Valerie snorted as she smothered her laughter with her palm, lifting her hand to lock arms with Helena who beamed back at her.

"Oh, if only," Valerie sighed.

THEY ARRIVED BACK at Audrey and Valerie's flat at a late hour, late enough to encourage Helena to stay in the extra bedroom disguised as Valerie's to deter close-minded visitors. After soaking herself in a lukewarm bath and the gaze of candlelight, Helena stepped from the deep bathtub and onto the soft bathmat. Slipping into the white dressing gown borrowed from Audrey, Helena turned to face the mirror dangling over the basin. She checked the leathery scar that began to coat her skin, the dim candlelight doing little to improve the sight of her hands and upper chest, or the twisting insecurity that churned her stomach.

A slight sound tore her from her sinking insecurity, growing into faint muffling of giggles and high-pitched notes of a music box. Tying the thin dressing gown, Helena crept towards the bathroom door, nudged it open to peer out the thin gap, down the hallway and into the dim living room. A pair of silhouettes bobbed behind the glow of the candle on the coffee table, dancing with the flickering shadows in tune to the music box. Helena's lips jerked into a brief smile as she watched Audrey and Valerie waltz about the room, captured in one another's eyes as soft smiles grew on their faces. Slipping from the bathroom, Helena darted across the thin hallway into her temporary bedroom, closing the door to preserve their privacy.

## CHAPTER 13

*H*elena felt surrounded in a thick fog of fatigue, smothered behind her heavy eyelids as she searched her desk for her grandmother's ring. She had trouble focusing with her latest reoccurring nightmare floating in the back of her head. She'd stand in a circle of black fire, the outlines of screaming faces emerging from the thick smoke before turning to ash at her feet. Silent shrieks tore her throat before the fire would swarm around a distant figure, a man with a face Helena would never forget as his eyes melted in their sockets before pouring out on his cheeks, a pair of needle-like hands replacing them. She would wake up coated in cold sweat and shivering beneath her covers until the first beam of morning light brought her from the darkness.

After rummaging through another desk drawer, she shoved it closed with a bitter huff. She took in a deep breath, calming the swelling ocean inside her before leaving her office to find Audrey in the chapel, setting up for the afternoon's funeral.

"Audrey, have you seen my ring?" she asked.

"Last I saw it was on your finger," Audrey replied, arching her eyebrows in concern.

"It must be at home," Helena said, rubbing her strained eyes.

Audrey frowned at her, stepping towards her with a soft gaze.

"Are you al—"

Her query collapsed beneath the clap of the chapel doors that swung open to reveal Christian as he stormed inside, his hands clenched and eyes fixated on Helena. Valerie followed, gripping her skirts as she sped past him to park beside Audrey. Helena frowned at Eric as he emerged from the hallway at a notably slow pace, his eyes sewed to the floor and his hands stuffed in his pockets before Christian spoke.

"So, you're arranging a funeral for Aunt Aubrey," he said, placing his hands on his hips.

Helena's eyes darted towards Eric who bit his lip as he felt the weight of her gaze.

"I'm sorry, I let it slip on the way here," he said.

"You should be sorry," Christian spat, aiming his twisted expression back towards Helena.

Helena tilted her head to the side, unable to absorb Christian's attempt at intimidation. It was as if she were watching an entitled little boy in the playground, his mock authority as weak as it was laughable.

"Who do you think you are sticking your nose in family business?" Christian barked.

Helena raised her eyebrows as she crossed her arms, keeping the silence as she glanced up and down Christian's figure heaving with fragile rage that was meant to threaten her.

"I was hired for a service and I am in the process of delivering it," she said with a concrete tone. "And I am always respectful of my clients' privacy."

"You're certainly not respectful, you didn't even consult me!" Christian spat.

"Ironically enough, not everything is about you, Christian," Eric muttered.

Christian's rage flew from Helena and towards Eric who rolled his eyes at Christian's crumbled snarl.

"I honestly don't see why you're throwing such a temper tantrum," Eric said. "You said you wanted nothing to do with her."

"Father said we are to have nothing to do with her," Christian replied, stepping to mirror Eric. "And you're wasting his money on her."

"Father's not here," Eric replied, drawing out his syllables in a cruel, childish manner.

"Don't you say that!" Christian barked.

Helena bit her lip as rotten emotion filled the room like a poisonous gas, the bitterness staining her tongue as she continued to watch.

"Enough, please!" Audrey said, stepping towards her older brothers. "She wouldn't want us to fight."

"I don't give a damn about that old hag, Audrey!" Christian said, twisting around to aim his whiny voice at her. "Honestly, how can you be so stupid!"

Audrey halted mid-step, freezing as if a bullet had shot through her chest. Her face wilted like a bruised flower, her eyes darting down. Helena bit her lip as a wave of anger arose from within her, her stiff jaw unlocking as she stepped towards Christian, her path blocked by a fiery bush of red hair.

"You're acting like children, both of you," Valerie spat. "Apologise to your sister, that was completely uncalled for, not to mention horribly cruel."

Eric bowed his head, biting his lip as he leaned back against his heels. Contrasting his twin brother, Christian stepped forward, his nostrils' flaring like a taunted bull.

"You're not my mother, what makes you think you can order me about?" Christian replied.

"Get out," Helena said, pushing down the boiling anger in her chest. "You've disrespected my clients and my employee. You are not welcome on my property."

"I can make you homeless with a single signature," Christian replied.

"You need two, he left the deed to both us, remember?" Eric said, his tone drained of emotion.

"I don't know why, all you do is scribble all day, you're pathetic," Christian spat.

Eric's face dropped, his eyes falling as Christian turned on his heel, his thunderous footsteps echoing through the room before he pulled the door shut with a heavy crash. Helena sighed as the tension eased from the room before glancing back towards Valerie and Audrey. Valerie kept her sharp eyes fixated on the door whilst gently holding Audrey's hand. Audrey chewed on her cheeks before lifting her eyes towards Eric who cleared his throat then muttered, "I'm sorry…to all of you."

Helena's eyebrows arched, a wave of sympathy flowing through her like a shot of bad medicine. Audrey stepped forward, still gripping Valerie's hand as she wrapped her opposite arm around Eric who buried his face between her neck and raised shoulder.

"Ignore him," Audrey said, "he's just trying to be like Father."

❧

FEELING SICKENED by the emotionally-poisoned air at the funeral home, Helena invited Eric back to the house, giving Audrey a deserved afternoon off with Valerie. They took seats on opposing couches, a gaping space between them as they rested against the respective arms of the sofas. The awkwardness had followed them, lingering through the room until they forced themselves into conversation.

"I'd originally come to tell you that my aunt will be arriving in a couple of weeks," Eric said. "Like I previously said, it takes a while for a letter to come from France, let alone someone's remains."

"That's all right, did she live in France for long?" Helena said, faking a bright tone.

"Most of her life, yes," Eric replied, keeping his eyes on the fireplace in front of him.

Helena sighed, dropping her friendly façade like a used handkerchief.

"If this is upsetting you, we can just find a middle ground and do a simple burial," Helena said.

"I think Christian won't mind that as much," Eric said, closing his eyes before tilting his face towards her. "Listen, it's not his fault for being so awful…I used to treat him terribly as a child, I was jealous of him because…"

Eric trailed off, his eyes on his lap as he bit his lip, his hand falling on the arm of the couch.

"Either way, I don't want you to think poorly of us," he said.

Helena bit her lip, her eyebrows knitted together as she lifted her hand, reaching towards Eric before placing her fingers across his wrist. Eric glanced up towards her, his face blank with heavy surprise. Helena swallowed before forcing her eyes on his to ensure her sincerity.

"If you hold no ill judgment against me, I'll do the same for you," she said.

Eric blinked, brightening warmth returning to his face. Helena grew a short smile before removing her hand from his wrist, leaning back into her seat whilst clearing her stiff throat. Amongst the quiet a heavy tapping moved through the house, disrupting the peaceful silence. Helena twisted around to glance about the room, unable to perfectly pin the origin of the blunt tapping.

"What is that?" Eric asked, his face creasing with thick irritation.

"I'll look," Helena said, lifting herself from the couch.

Going after her first assumption, Helena approached the front door, opening it to find the porch empty. Turning towards the kitchen, she halted in the open-door frame as she spotted the raven perched on the kitchen windowsill. She held her breath as it raked its beak against the glass, flinching with each sharp tap. A slight cold fell over her, her arms crossing over her chest as she attempted to shield herself from the rippling chills.

Stepping back from the kitchen, Helena turned around to face the foyer, the once prickling cold turning into frostbiting shock as her body tensed like a dry dishrag. In the centre of the foyer stood a misshapen figure with four trembling legs and two heads attached to limp necks. Helena couldn't tell if it was one man or technically two as the two ink-black bodies were sewn together by the guts, one lying diagonally across the other with a flat ribbon of twisted skin. Their blackened eyes bore into her, a midnight ocean swirling behind the soulless gloves. A duo of throaty moans emerged from their swollen lips as one of the four hands lifted towards her, acting as a lightning rod as another jolt of fear struck her.

"Did you find—"

As Eric stepped into the foyer, the conjoined men screamed, tripping over their distorted limbs as they stumbled backwards towards the front door. Helena clasped her hands over her gaping mouth as they let out a synchronised wail before falling against the floorboards, sinking through them as if they were a cloud of dust. Helena's eyes lingered over the now empty spot before she lifted them towards Eric who gawked down at the floor, his face twisted into a partial frown.

Helena's swelling shock disappeared as distant hope filled her chest like a candle inside a glass lantern.

"Did you see that?" she asked.

"N-see what?" he asked, dodging her glance. "What were you looking at?"

Helena's candle blew out, her lips curling inwards before muttering, "Nothing."

$\mathcal{T}$he deep chill of the late afternoon stabbed Helena's soft flesh as she stood outside Minerva's house, holding the wrapped present in hand as she knocked once again on the door. She tapped her heels against the porch as she waited, a smile spreading across her face as the door eased back, the smile quickly fading as she saw who stood behind it. Eight-year-old Hal stood with his fingers clutching the door handle, his dark eyes boring up at her with his lips twisted into a trembling frown.

"There's a man here, a policeman," he whispered.

Helena slipped inside the house, placing her hand on Hal's back as she bent down to whisper into his ear, "Go upstairs, I'll check on them."

Hal nodded before heading towards the stairs. Helena followed behind him as she neared the door to Minerva's office, the open frame allowing the muffled voices inside to spill into the hallway. Biting her lip, Helena glanced up towards the stairs to see Hal's loose frown staring down at her.

"It's okay, go on," she whispered, ensuring he finished his climb before moving on.

Helena pressed her palm against the wall, pressing her feet lightly against the floor as she crept towards the room. Through the open door, she saw Henry sitting in the corner of the room in a wooden dining chair, his dark skin clinging to his meatless bones as he stared out of Helena's viewing range. His skeletal fingers clutched the arms of the chair as the faceless voices continued to converse in front of him, the tension as thick and poisonous as a toxic gas.

Helena wavered in the corner of his vision until he tilted his face towards her, biting his lip before glancing back towards his original point. She listened to the bitter exchange, venomous dread flushing though her as she attached the familiar voices to their owners.

"I'm not getting involved in this, Mr Jude," Minerva said, her soft breath hiding a dark undertone.

"Detective Inspector Jude," he replied.

"You said you were off duty."

Henry shifted in his seat, clearing his blocked throat to nudge his way into the conversation.

"Sir, I still don't understand why you're here," Henry said beneath his crackling voice.

There was thick silence, causing Helena to stiffen herself into complete stillness, her anxiety of exposure prickling beneath her skin.

"You are friends with Miss Morrigan, correct?" Jude asked.

"I knew her grandparents, we're all in the same business," Minerva replied.

"Have you ever noticed something strange or odd about her?"

Helena's body trembled, her mind painting an image of the wet smile Jude would've worn asking that question.

"No, she's a bit of a spitfire at times, but she's a good

woman," Minerva replied. "I'd leave her with my son without question."

"Are you sure about that?"

Helena's ears perked as rustling came from the room, followed by a faint wiping sound as if he were sliding a piece of paper across a desk surface. Brief silence followed, keeping Helena hovered in trembling suspense.

"I already know about all of this," Minerva said.

"Really?" Jude asked, his voice crumbling with his devious intentions.

"Yes," Minerva replied, a high-pitched zip coming from the zoom as she presumably slipped the paper back towards him. "Now, I have work to do, Detective Inspector...and you have no reason to barge into my home like you own me."

Another silence followed, lingering behind Minerva's brave response before a blunt rumbling of a chair against wooden floorboards shattered the once vivid hope within the room.

"Yet," Jude replied.

A trail of heavy thumps charged towards her, her body jolting as tight fear clasped her throat. She remained where she stood, facing the door, her posture stiff, as Jude strode from the office, a choppy gasp emerging from his broken smirk. Helena sharpened her gaze, jerking her eyebrow before marching past him.

"I'll be talking to you soon, Miss Morrigan," he said.

"You won't find me here," Helena replied, pausing by the door frame to glance back at him, "so there's no reason for you to return."

Jude tugged on his jacket, razors sticking from his piercing pupils as he sliced her with one final glare. With a horse-like humph, he turned on his heel, storming from the house like a disappointed restaurant patron. Helena sighed before sliding into the study, aiming a faint smile at

Henry as he slouched in his seat, biting his dry lips. Helena swallowed as she approached Minerva's desk, watching as her friend hid her face in her palms. She waited as Minerva sighed lifting her face to gaze up at her, her hands clasped together on the surface of the desk.

"Helena…" she said. "I am so lucky to have everything that I have. I worked my entire life, my parents and their parents worked…I have a child, my husband's sick, my business, he could…"

"It's okay, you don't have to explain," Helena replied, dipping her chin towards her chest. "This looks really bad on my part and I understand that…"

"I know you haven't hurt anyone, you never have and you never will," Minerva replied.

Helena nodded biting her lip as a paralysing sting punched her chest, filling it like an injection of numbness. She set the wrapped present onto Minerva's desk, flinching as Minerva reached over to place her hand over hers, wrapping her fingers around Helena's palm before giving it a light squeeze.

"I'm sorry," she said.

HELENA FOUGHT WITH HER UMBRELLA, the wind threatening to tear it from her grip as she stood before the newly erected gravestone, her opposite arm hooked around Audrey as she mourned over her aunt's grave.

*'Aubrey Hart, 1796 – 1855'*

A few distant relatives sent their regards, but nothing of overt significance. As the rain pummelled down on them like tiny bullets from the rumbling clouds, Helena remained, waiting with iron patience before Audrey was ready. As they turned to follow the aisle between tombstones, Helena caught the sight of

*'Matthew Christian Tarter, 1795 – 1855*
*Husband of Ada nee Hart, 1799 – 1844*
*Father of Eric, Christian and Audrey.'*

She squinted at the name before it faded beneath the curtains of rain, burying it into the back of her mind before she glanced ahead at a distant figure jogging towards them. Helena lifted the umbrella to allow Eric to slide beneath, the rim of his hat overflowing with water, his pale skin freckled with raindrops.

"The carriage is bogged, there'd be no point in trying," he shouted over the roar of the rain.

Helena glanced to her side, unable to see the house from behind the heavy mist that clouded the fields. Yet the needle-like chill of the cold wind willed her to find shelter beneath a dry roof.

"Could you manage a decent stroll?" she asked.

THE STORM CONTINUED like heavy gunfire outside, the lightning like bombs spreading white flashes through the bruised sky. Helena's body continued to ripple with icy chills as the house sunk into a deep freeze. After collecting two spare blankets and matching pillows from the wardrobe, Helena knocked on the second bedroom door, biting her lip as the thunder growled at her from behind the walls of the house.

"Come in!" Audrey called.

Helena entered to find Audrey bent over a three-fingered candle holder, nursing the enflamed match with her hand as she passed it from candlewick to candlewick. She smiled at her before crossing the room to place the pile of blankets and pillows on the naked bed. The second unused bedroom was a mirror image of Helena's except for the small set of drawers that replaced Helena's towering wardrobe and darkened blue shade to the walls.

"Valerie will be worried about me," Audrey sighed, twisting her wrist to fan out the match.

"We'll take her out tomorrow, make it up to her," Helena replied, grinning before laying one of the blankets over the bare mattress, smoothing it down with her flat palms.

"Thank you," Audrey said.

Audrey sucked on her cheeks, her soft eyes soaring across the room to survey the light-hungry shadows squashed into the corners of the ceiling, hiding beneath the chest of drawers and under the rickety bed. The thunder outside rumbled like a monster's belly as a lock of her warm blonde hair fell over her pale face.

"I always hated this house, even when I was little," she said, pinching her fingers with the opposite hand. "It has a…loneliness to it. No matter what, you feel like no one is here."

"I'm right next door if you need anything," Helena replied, arching her eyebrows.

"No, I'm sorry, I'm just being silly," Audrey replied with a bashful smile.

Helena produced a close-lipped grin, gathering the remaining pillow and blanket before turning back to Audrey.

"Good night," she said.

"Good night," Audrey replied.

Stepping from the room, Helena closed the door behind her, flinching as another branch of lightning struck from the clouds. Helena caught her breath, sucking it in before releasing it. Descending the darkened staircase, Helena followed a new light flickering from the living room like a campfire in a wide field. She found Eric spread out on the couch, his long limbs partially hidden by the shadows that barred the light from the single candle on the end table by his feet.

"I thought you might like these," she said.

Eric pushed himself off the couch, the warm glow clinging to his face as he stepped forward to take the blanket and pillow from her.

"Thank you," he said.

"Are you sure you don't want the spare room?" she asked. "Audrey and I could share."

"No, I'd hate to bother you," he replied, dipping his gaze down, leaving thick silence before them. "I'd been meaning to ask. Are you sure everything is all right with Jude?"

"Oh, no, it's just…"

Helena lowered her eyes, biting her lip as the worry swirled in her chest, unlocking the mental seal behind her lips.

"He scares me," she said. "I worry about him…he thinks I've done something wrong."

"Well," Eric said, teasing his bottom lip with his teeth, "if he's careless enough to gamble away all his savings, I'm sure he's stupid enough to think that."

The right corner of Helena's lips dug up into her cheek before the spark in her chest faded as quickly as it struck.

"I could talk to him if you like," Eric said. "He knew my father, so he should listen to me…probably."

"What could you say?" Helena asked.

"You're harassing a perfectly good woman, sir," he replied with a thin smile.

"Thank you."

"Your hands," he said.

The warmth drained from Helena's face as she acknowledged the soft air that caressed the scars covering her bare hands. Her eyes flared as she recalled taking them off due to habit as she stepped inside the dry house. Locking her hands behind her back, she thought back to

Audrey, assuming she mustn't have noticed before gazing up at Eric.

"I'm sorry," he said, "I shouldn't have mentioned it."

"That's all right," she mumbled, tilting her head towards the dancing flame beside her. "It's just from a fire when I was little."

"I have a scar on my back from when I fell into a rose bush," Eric said, arching his eyebrow in slight desperation.

"How did you fall?" Helena asked.

"I didn't technically fall...Christian pushed me," he replied.

Helena sealed her lips as she huffed a half-chuckle, a smile spreading across her chin.

"That doesn't sound like him at all," she said.

Her smile shrunk to a blank line as Eric reached towards her, his fingers tracing her elbows before trailing down her forearms and towards her wrist. She held her breath as he drew her toffee-paper hands toward him, her brow creasing as churning suspicion curled in her chest.

"Thank you for letting us stay, we would've had to walk for almost an hour out there," he said with a soft smile.

Helena's lips curled into a slight smirk as she gazed up at him thorough squinted eyelids.

"You're wel—"

A standing ovation of lightning clapped through her response, the white flashes pouring through the windows like bursts of violent sunlight. Helena jolted, squeezing Eric's hands as she slid her foot towards him, hiding in the shadow of his frame. An image flashed before her eyes with the second strike of lightning, the whirring of electricity buzzing off tiled walls and the dark figures standing over her. A slight squeak escaped her throat as she pressed her cheek against Eric's chest, cramming her eyes shut as she tried to escape her snapping memories. Eric's warmth breathed on her as he released her hands before wrapping his arms around her back, his chin resting on the tip of her head as she clutched his black waistcoat.

"It's okay," Eric whispered softly.

Helena bit her lip, pressing her nose against his chest as she buried herself deeper within, running from the monsters that lived inside, her body trembling from the inner battle. She gasped as she eventually came up for air, the fear lodging in her chest as she regained loose stability.

"Are you all right?" Eric asked. "Do you need anything?"

"I just need to go to bed," Helena mumbled, removing her damp cheek from Eric's chest, moulding away from him like a disconnected puzzle piece.

Eric stepped back, lowering his hands from her back to the bend of her shoulders, staring down at her with half his face dipped in darkness, the other glowing in the light of the candle.

"I'm just down here…and Audrey's next door," he said.

"Thank you," she said, a sheet of mortification falling over her like a black veil. "Goodnight."

"Goodnight."

## CHAPTER 15

*C*overed in a thick shawl, Valerie leaned over the coffee table in the centre of the living room, her eyes worn and bloodshot having stayed up waiting for Audrey. The rain continued to fall, hitting the pavement like bullets against tin. She imagined that she'd stayed with her brothers or with Helena, yet a common concern plagued her, nudging her from sleep like a feverish cold.

A single candle burned on the edge of the coffee table, creating a fuzzy orange circle that bled out into thick blackness. A pile of crumpled parchment piled at her feet, countless attempts she'd thrown out as she couldn't perfect her message. She tapped the tip of the pen to her lips, reading over the most important piece she'd ever written.

*'Dearest,*

*Ever since our first meeting you have supported me, and you loved me without condition, which is more than I could ever ask for. So, I would be honoured if you would spend the rest of your life with me, in whatever form that may take.*

*This may seem impossible, but I have a hard time imagining it any other way, unless of course, you don't feel ready. I know you worry, but if worst comes to worst, we can go to France like*

*we discussed. I hope it would never come to that, but there's little
I wouldn't do for you.*

*Regardless of what would happen now or in the future, I will
love you. That is my promise to you.*

*Val'*

She bit her lip as she considered rewriting it once again
when a faint creak came from the stairwell outside,
followed by another sharper squeak.

"Audrey?" she called, folding the letter and pushing
herself from the couch.

Opening the door, she dipped her head into the darkened hallway with little light spilling in from the living
room. Even beneath her shawl, Valerie felt a solid chill
ripple through her, her body tensing as she peered through
the thick curtains of darkness. With throbbing tenseness in
her chest, Valerie eased the door closed, unable to shake it
as she stepped away to find the key to lock it. A faint
whoosh shot to her ears, her pace halting as she began to
twist around, her action snagging as a jolt of fear rushed
through her veins, her lips forming into an open frown as a
firm hand clasped over her mouth.

## CHAPTER 16

*H*elena climbed the staircase towards Audrey's apartment with a bag full of freshly baked bread and bottled jam from the neighbouring bakery, the warm smell wafting into her nose. She held the key to the flat between her fingers as Audrey conversed with the postman outside. As she reached the peak of the stairs, her mind wandered back to Eric who'd walked back to his father's house that morning, leaving her with a conflicting tug within her, the kindness he's shown almost foreign to her. Painting a smile on her face, Helena knocked on the door with the key clenched in her fist.

"Valerie, it's Helena!" she said, adjusting her grip on the parcel of bread. "Audrey and I brought breakfast!"

Helena counted to ten, waiting for a response, her impatience biting her as she inserted the key into the lock, pushing open the door with a slight nudge.

"Valerie?" she called.

Helena sealed her lips as the stillness of the room wafted out into the hallway, instinctive dread hovering over her as she gripped the bread like a teddy bear. The drawn curtains blocked the morning sun, casting blurry darkness across the room. Helena left the door open as she took a step deeper into the room, treading on the pieces of paper that layered the floor and the smell of the melted candle glued to the coffee table tickling her nostrils. Placing the paper bag of bread next to the fallen candle, she then stepped towards the hallway to find the mirrored bedroom doors wedged open but the bathroom door sealed shut. Helena swallowed the swelling lump in her throat as she tumbled down the dark tunnel, grasping the cold doorknob.

A single candle sat on the basin, melted to a stub and flickering in the fresh air. Helena shivered as the tiles glowed in the soft light, her eyes scanning the shadow-infected room until they landed on the bathtub. Helena's body tensed, a crippling cold rushing through her as the clear red liquid sparkled in the dim light. Valerie lay face down in the water, her white nightgown covering her like a damp cloud, concealing her bare skin that turned a cherry red beneath the window of watered-down blood, the orange freckles on her shoulders turning black like blood clots as she floated like a poisoned fish.

"Audrey! Audrey!" Helena screamed.

Helena launched forward, dipping her hands into the cold water as she gripped Valerie's arms, a slash of water ran down the front of her dress as she flipped Valerie over. Her blood shot through her like shards of glass through a vacuum, her desperation smothered by a choking shock as she glanced back down into the tub, a scream lodged in her constricting throat.

Valerie's face was an octopus blue, her skin wet and clammy from the water, her silky red hair spread out like a goddess's halo and her body rocking in the reactive waves like a baby in a cradle. Yet she was physically empty, open like a velvet jewellery box from the arch of her collarbones to the bottom of her navel.

❧

HELENA SAT like a stuffed doll in the hallway, her shoulder doing little to smother Audrey's wails. Helena wrapped her arms around Audrey's back, fighting her weight as she slumped over her like a heavy blanket, clutching Helena's waist as if it were the edge of a cliff. Helena left the tears dry on her face, the new ones adding additional layers before she'd lick the few that trailed along her lips. Inside the apartment stood a collection of uniformed police officers who had barred Audrey from her own home as they gathered evidence, leaving Helena to explain briefly that her partner was gone.

The door to the flat opened, the curtains still drawn to further conceal the horrors inside. Jude stepped outside, bringing a certain dread with him like an overpowering cologne.

"You have to let me in there!" Audrey screamed, her face burning red and glistening wet with tears like a washed apple. "Please, I have to see her, she's in there all alone!"

"Would you please calm down, Miss Tarter?" Jude sighed, his empty tone injecting Helena with masking rage. "Miss Morrigan, did you happen to touch the body when you entered the room?"

"I thought she was drowning," she replied.

"Well, you can't drown without any lungs," Jude grumbled.

Helena's chest capsized, tightening like a lock as she glanced towards Audrey whose watery eyes swelled upon hearing the first detail of Valerie's death. Helena grasped Audrey as she attempted to stand, wrestling her back into her grip as Audrey resumed her rainstorm of tears, screaming at Jude as she lay on Helena's lap.

"What do you mean! Don't say that! No! No! No!" she

wailed, her voice softening as she began to chant. "If I had been here, if I had been here, if I had been here."

"Audrey?"

Helena glanced down the stairs, the morning sun covering the figure that sprinted up the flight of steps. Eric fell to his knees beside Helena, gathering Audrey in his arms as she locked her arms around his neck, crying into his collarbone.

"What happened?" he asked.

"If you come inside, Mr Tarter, I'd be happy to explain," Jude said, stepping from the door frame, gesturing inside the apartment with a wave of his flat palm. "You'll have to forgive the scenery since there are no other private places available at the moment."

"I'm busy right now," Eric replied through gritted teeth.

"It's important, trust me," Jude replied. "And I'm sure you don't want to upset her more by discussing it directly in front of her."

Eric bit his lip, glancing towards Helena as if searching for confidence. Helena nodded, aiming her icy glare towards Jude as Eric passed Audrey to her as if she were a newborn baby. Despite his reactive scowl, Helena kept her eyes fixated on Jude as he let Eric inside, closing the door with a blunt thud.

"Come on, let's go downstairs," Helena whispered.

As Audrey's whimpering quieted, Helena pulled her to her feet, looping her knotted arms around her neck as she embraced Audrey's waist, guiding her towards the stairs. She paused as she levelled with the apartment door, stepping sideways to aim her ear on it, picking up the quiet mutterings of the gentlemen on the other side.

"Do you even understand the meaning of the word 'sympathy'? Isn't that desired in your line of work?" Eric said.

"I'm not going to put on a show to please others," Jude replied, "unlike your friend out there."

"Would you just leave her alone?" Eric hissed. "She's here comforting my sister as if she were her own, doesn't that stir you at all?"

"I'm just doing my job, you should be grateful," Jude replied. "I'm sure your father taught you to be as such."

"Not in the way he desired," Eric replied.

The door swung open, revealing a red-faced Eric who skidded to a blunt stop upon locking eyes with Helena, his expression falling from a tense glare to a blank stare.

"Are you coming?" she asked.

THE GAPING ROOMS of the Tarter residence gave Helena little ease, the climbing walls standing over her like prison walls. She held a warm cup of tea in her palms, pretending to sip at it as her stomach growled with violent disobedience. The glands in the front of her throat swelled, her mouth sour like used bathwater. She imagined Audrey in her childhood room upstairs flung over her bed whilst crying into her pillow.

Helena occupied herself from her trembling by watching Eric walk back and forth the length of the room, passing his various paintings as he stared at the toes of his shoes. Her eyes followed him, her body flinching every time her thoughts would wander back towards Audrey or the sight of Valerie's soulless body. Interrupting his continuous pattern, Eric spun around with a violent twist, facing Helena with arched brows.

"They were together, weren't they?" he asked.

Helena glanced down towards her tea, leaning forward to place it on the rim of the desk.

"That's not for me to say," she said.

Eric nodded before wandering towards the window as he drew his hands down his face, dragging the loose skin of his cheeks. Helena's eyes drifted back to her lap as the silence sunk in, her body slumping as the images of Valerie returned. Her eyes burned as a wall of tears climbed up her irises, falling down her cheeks as she began to tremble, choking on the clogging sobs in her throat. Beneath her cries, she heard several blunt taps before a heavy presence hovered over her, a soft hand falling on her shoulder.

"I'm sorry," she whispered.

"No, it's all right," Eric said. "Here."

Helena continued to hiccup between heaving sobs as Eric kneeled beside the chair, coiling his arms around her. Helena filled the space, resting her head on his shoulder, hiding her face in her palms as she shook, tears staining her cheeks as she snuffled out the endless waves that drowned her. She buried herself in Eric's embrace with no judgment or price pushing her away until she became an empty shell slumped against him. Her sobs slowed into steady breathing as she drew herself back together lifting her chin on Eric's shoulder, taking in a breath of cold air.

"Any better?" Eric asked.

"Slightly," she said. "We'd better go check on Audrey."

Helena lifted her face from his shoulder, freezing as her cheek brushed against his. Red heat flushed her face as she drew back, her lips wedged open as she fell into the gaze of his dark brown eyes. Gawking up at her, Eric swallowed, his Adam's apple rolling in his throat as he shifted his head a centimetre towards her as a polite proposition. Helena held her breath as she tilted her head downwards, closing her eyes as she pressed her lips against his. The tension eased from her body, an intoxicating lightness that flushed out some of the heaviness clinging to her expanding chest.

Helena's fluttering stomach faded as she leaned backwards, the fresh air tickling her throat as she gazed down at Eric. Natural awkwardness followed as they detached from each other's embrace, faint red pinching their cheeks.

"Um, yes, good idea," he said, rising to his feet.

Helena cleared her throat as she followed him from the study, brushing against his elbow as they turned to climb up the marble staircase. The second story mirrored the downstairs layered in white and cream-coloured walls, but instead wooden panels lined the floor and red curtains framed the windows. Approaching Audrey's bedroom door, Helena tapped her knuckles against the thick wood, glancing towards Eric before calling out.

"Audrey, it's us!"

"I-I want to be alone!"

Audrey sounded as if she were consumed by a disease, her voice weak and nasally whilst pouring out a thick accent of pain. Helena flinched as the second-hand misery cut into her like a jagged knife, nausea numbing her throat.

"That's all right, we're just downstairs if you need anything," Eric said.

Helena sucked on her lips as she glanced back at Eric before they retraced their steps down the hallway. A distant figure emerged from the staircase, pausing as they noticed them before meeting them in the centre of the hallway. Christian's eyes darted towards them, giving them a slight nod before passing them.

"I assume you've heard about...what's happened?" Helena asked.

Christian paused, his foot hovering mid-step before he twisted back towards them. His eyes drifted to the carpet before lifting up towards Eric, his thin lips parting before he mumbled like a tired child.

"I'll be going back to university tomorrow. Will you be able to look after her?"

Helena's eyes rolled in their sockets, her low expectations deprived as she glared back at Christian. She felt the bitterness breathe off Eric like a cologne as she stood beside him, fuelling her own consuming disgust.

"As if you're capable of doing so anyway," Eric muttered.

Christian bowed his head like a scolded puppy before re-emerging with a pouting glare, "Well, at least—"

"Don't," Helena snapped. "She'll hear you."

Helena reached up to squeeze Eric's arm, jerking her head towards the stairs before stepping towards it with a concrete stare. Eric sighed before following her down the staircase, taking her hand as she lowered it from his arm.

"I'll stay if you need me to," she said.

"Thank you," he replied.

## CHAPTER 17

*T*rapped in a blanket of black, Helena twisted and tugged in an attempt to free herself. Her silent screams passed through her lips, her throat straining as she failed to muster a single sound. The skin covering her hands began to prickle before building up to a festering burn, flames flicking from behind her fingernails before they burst into blazes like stubborn candles. Helena tried to smother them in her night gown, the fabric burning away into blackened flecks that blended with the darkness.

Her hands began to crumble, falling to specks of ash that glowed in front of her, merging like a hoard of butterflies until it formed the vision of a man, completing him fully except for the empty eye sockets. Helena trembled, the pain pulsing through her body increasing as she gazed over the blackened corpse before it gradually began to shift, his hips expanding and chest swelling, the fire latching to his head to create long locks of red. Helena's breath left her lungs as she stared back at Valerie quaking as a gallon of red-stained water flowed from her gaping mouth.

A scream racked up Helena's throat like nails clawing at

a chalkboard, the sound releasing the horror building in her chest as she flew out of her covers. She shielded her eyes with her palms as she pressed her forehead against the bend of her knees. She heaved as she tried to force herself back to reality, still emotionally glued to the nightmare.

Lifting her eyes from her trembling fingers, Helena inspected the darkness of her bedroom, her eyes darting from corner to corner until she caught a shadow hovering in the centre of the room. The black spot began to grow at the foot of her bed, drawing in the darkness of the room before it formed into a tall figure. First came the long-buried professor gawking at her, his strawy beard stained with black blood. Helena pressed her back against the frame of the bed, her ankles digging into the mattress as two heads grew out of the professor's open stomach. Helena gagged as the professor capsized like an outwards sock, folding inwards so that the conjoined university students could grow out of him like a parasite. Mr Little and Mr Jordan groaned as they stumbled against one another, raising their respective hands towards her as they took a step forward. Helena slid up the wall, her feet sinking into the mattress as she stood up. The university students' faces began to melt away, their clouded eyes glowing a triggering red, their intertwining stomachs merging together as their moaning turned into a heavy growl. Helena swallowed her breath.

"Leave me alone!" she yelled.

The twisting transformation paused, a new figure solidifying amongst the flipping clump of bodies, a familiar head emerging from behind the red-eyed skull. Foreman stood before her, his rotting jaw wedged open as he gazed at her through clouded eyes. Helena's feat stabilized, her thrumming heart knocking against her rib cage as she gawked at him. Foreman attempted to speak, his dead voice box managing only a strong moan before backing away into the darkness.

With her hair soaked in cold rainwater, Helena descended the stairs after a quick wash. Her arms pulsed in exhaustion after hours of assembling a new coffin, stray flakes of sawdust peppering her clothes as she re-entered the kitchen. She found Eric bent over the new coffin, the sleeves of his white dress shirt rolled up past his elbows as his forearms freckled with paint. Helena rounded the island bench as Eric pulled away, paintbrush in hand, to examine his work. A white dove sat in the corner of the lid, graced with fluttering white wings and a golden crown of laurel leaves circling its smooth body.

"That looks amazing," she said, leaning her cheek against his arm.

She smiled as she felt his lips embrace her hairline. She pressed her face against the stiff fabric of his shirt as he wrapped his arm around her. The fuzzy thrumming in her chest faded as a blunt knock called her from the front door.

"That'd be Audrey," she said, slipping away from Eric with a smile.

He grinned back at her as she left the kitchen, crossing the foyer to open the front door. The smile dropped from her face like a picture from a wall as her eyes darted between the two contrasting figures standing before her.

"Detective Jude," she said.

"Detective Inspector," Jude corrected. "May we come in?"

Helena's eyes darted towards Audrey who raised her shoulders in a brief shrug. She stepped aside drawing the door back with her as Jude and Audrey slipped inside.

Swallowing a fleshy lump in her throat, she glanced towards the kitchen doorframe as Eric emerged removing the paint off his hand with a cloth and gazing at her beneath a creased brow.

"I have guests, so if you would please make this quick," Helena said to Jude with a blunt snap of the closing door.

"I'm sure it will be," he said with a grin.

Centring herself in the middle of the foyer, Helena crossed her arms as Jude pulled a pair of files from his jacket pocket, placing one in each hand, holding one out towards her.

"Could you tell me what it is?" he asked.

Helena glanced towards Audrey and Eric who'd moved to stand beside his sister by the living room door, before reaching for the file. She clasped it in both hands before she read over the title stamped on the beige cover. Her blood ran cold, her joints locking as a flash of panic rushed through her. Reeling herself back in, she claimed the shaky ocean inside as she replied.

"It's a medical record, or a summary of such."

"Yes, could you read it out for me?" Jude asked, a smile growing on his face.

Helena clenched her teeth, her eyes lingering over the file as she felt Eric and Audrey's eyes hovering over her.

"Helena, are you all right?" Audrey asked.

"She knows how to read," Jude said, denting his sunny tone before grinning back at Helena.

Helena sighed, pinching the cover before flipping it open, her mouth souring as she gazed over the top of the page, gripping the paper to try and squeeze back her dread.

"Name: Helena Mara Morrigan, age: fifteen, sex: female..." she said, pausing before glancing back up at Jude. "This is a private document, if we could—"

"Why?" Jude asked, his face dropping into faux confusion. "Do you have something to hide?"

"I'm not playing your game," Helena replied, her tone as sharp as her glare.

"If you are making her uncomfortable, you need to leave," Eric said.

"This is police business, Tarter," Jude barked, returning his stone-cold gaze towards Helena. "Go on."

Helena bit her lip, debating whether or not to speak it for herself or have Jude twist the facts on the chart. Helena resumed, stumbling over her sentences as if she were dancing on slippery ice.

"Paranoid Schizophrenia, admitted age seven by maternal aunt. Refuses medication and treatment...no proven history of violence...released: 1847 to maternal grandparents."

Snapping closed the binder, Helena glared up at Jude whose wet grin returned to his tilted chin.

"If you're bent on simply humiliating me, it hasn't worked," she said.

"What kind of a woman has a fascination with death?" Jude asked.

Helena frowned at the question she'd heard so many times before, yet the tone did not match. There was no arrogance or amusement, there was suspicion and a dark undertone that made her heart thrum in her chest, knocking against the bars of her ribcage.

"Does it say violent on this chart?" she asked, holding the file out towards him.

"I also have this," he said, holding up the forgotten file. "It's a police report."

Helena held her breath, her lips sealed shut as she watched Jude flip open the binder, vulnerable helplessness skimming over her prickled skin.

"October 30th, 1840. Forty-five-year-old male found tortured and burned in his home, his eyes gouged out of his skull," Jude said.

Helena's eyes darted towards Eric and Audrey who stood with her hand clasped over her gaping mouth.

"One witness: the victim's seven-year-old niece who claimed that a dead man tried to steal her uncle's soul... now that's one heck of childhood imagination," Jude finished, glancing up towards her with an arched brow.

"And if you read the full report you would know that they never caught the assailant," Helena said, tossing the hospital file back towards him.

Jude gasped in a flash of shock, fumbling with the file. He sharpened his glare as he cleared his throat.

"Well, that's because they never investigated you," he said.

"Yes, a seven-year-old child set her own uncle on fire and scooped out his eyes," Helena said, rolling her eyes despite the lump swelling in her throat.

"Perhaps not an ordinary child," he said.

Jude stepped forward, the files falling from his hands as he got closer to Helena, gripping the fabric of her gloves.

"No!" Helena screamed.

"Stop that!" Audrey snapped.

Jude kept a tight grip on Helena's hands as he attempted to drag the fabric from her scars, drawing her left glove down her wrist as Eric shoved him backwards. Audrey wrapped her arms around Helena as she shivered, the alight figure of her uncle flashing over her eyes, his strained screams echoing through her ears. She didn't dare shut her eyes, afraid of opening them and finding him kneeling before her with her mother's fingers sinking into his eye sockets.

"I-I tried to save him...I was traumatised and now I am recovered," Helena said, struggling to maintain the strength in her voice as the memories came flooding back.

A tear rolled down her eye, her gloves dangling from her fingers like clothes on a washing line. Audrey wrapped her hand around Helena's wrist, tugging the gloves back to fit Helena whilst ignoring the thick scars presented to her.

"It's all right, it's okay," she cooed.

Jude sorted like a panting horse, his eyes darting between Eric and Audrey as they glared back at him with thick disgust. Helena lifted her eyes back towards him as he straightened his jacket, clearing his throat before turning to Eric.

"Mr Tarter?" Jude asked.

Eric blinked as if struck with heavy daze.

"Yes?" he replied.

"Has Miss Morrigan been…seeing things that aren't there, speaking to thin air…or anything like that?" Jude asked.

Eric's lips wedged open with no words waiting behind them.

"I've spoken to your brother," Jude said. "He claims that Miss Morrigan exposed herself to him whilst he visited her."

"What?" Eric said, his wide eyes darting towards Helena.

"He walked in on me!" Helena spat.

"It is clear you have hatred of men," Jude said, crossing his arms as he took a step towards her.

"I don't hate you," she said, restraining her bubbling rage. "I just won't tolerate you."

Jude's stone face melted, his lips tilting into a frown as he leaned backwards. He shook his head, flicking off his confusion before resuming his assault.

"You kill them, don't you?" he continued. "For satisfaction, for thrill, your bodies in the funeral home aren't enough clearly."

"Of course not!" she exclaimed, failing to hide her hurt.

"You are basing everything off of circumstance," Audrey said, her arms still wrapped around Helena.

"She's right, you have no proof," Eric said.

"Oh really," Jude replied, reaching into his inner jacket pocket.

He pulled out two large plastic bags with 'evidence' printed across the top. Inside the first was a piece of parchment with ink splattered across the surface, the second had a silver ring with a glistening black jewel. Helena's blood ran cold as her eyes fixated on the ring, her finger twitching as Jude took a step towards her.

"Do you recognise this, Miss Morrigan?" he asked.

"Where did you get that?" Helena asked, her voice brittle.

"It was found in the bottom of Miss Valerie Wolfe's bath," he replied. "I think I might muster up a motive."

Jude's words swallowed Helena like an ocean wave. He hovered the second plastic bag in front of his face, reading aloud the ink-coated letter inside.

"Dearest. Ever since our first meeting you have supported me, and you loved me without condition, which is more than I could ever ask for."

Helena frowned, her eyes squinting as Jude tilted his head and held the letter up for her to see.

"I saw you two together, having dinner," he said. "This was meant for you, was it not?"

Helena's eyes darted sideways towards Audrey who'd taken a step back from her, her hand resting on her shoulder. Helena bit her lip as Audrey's doe eyes flashed with a glaze of panic, darting between Helena and Jude with open lips.

"It was," Helena lied, chiming in before Audrey could. "But what does that have to do with anything?"

"It proves your hatred of men and perhaps that you clearly cannot control your urges, you would kill your own lover," he said, tucking the letter back into his shirt pocket.

"Oh, come on," Helena replied, rolling her eyes in exasperation.

Jude bent down to gather the dropped files, placing both back into his opposite jacket pocket before stepping towards Helena, his rotten breath prickling her face as she shrunk beneath his gaze.

"I have another three policemen outside," he said. "Will you come quietly?"

Helena bit her lips, tears swelling in her eyes as her body began to tremble. Her seven-year-old self screamed inside her, begging her to not let another uniformed figure take her away again. She held her breath, her eyes fixated on the floor to hide another disobedient tear that retreated down her cheek.

"I have done nothing, I have nothing to fear," she said, more so to herself than to Jude.

As soon as the words left her lips, Jude's rough hand gripped her upper arm, tearing her from Audrey's embrace and towards the door.

"I don't think that's necessary," Audrey gasped, her voice squeaking like an old swing.

Helena bowed her head, her internal darkness consuming her as she opened the gates behind her eyes, tears rolling down as Jude swung open the door, the cold air slapping her skin before she was shoved out of her own home.

HELENA'S BREATH bubbled in her chest, her lungs burning as she walked by the aisles of cells. Tears streamed down her cheeks, the soft voice of her grandmother whispering in her ear 'you'll never be locked up again, no one will ever take you away again'. The broken promise tore her to pieces, her toes dragging against the concrete floor, her armpits straining as two officers lifted her by her elbows.

As she passed each cell, a flash of blinding light shunned her, dipping her in and out of heavy delusion. Each ray of light created a window back into the asylum, the pale green hallways, orchestra of strained moans and the cast of figures from the pale-face patients, the brawny doctors and the silent nurses.

She felt as if she were bobbing in water, her arms restrained and legs strained from kicking as the water pressed against her lips and nose. The hard tug of the officer's hands turned into the strong arms of the ocean, rocking her, drowning her into submission.

udrey sat slumped over the couch in Helena's living room, a dry thunder storm rumbling around her as if she were sitting inside an empty stomach. Her mind raced with trickling anxiety, her thoughts swarming her mind like flies over a pile of meat. Resting her palm in her hand, she glanced over towards the opposite couch where Christian sat biting his lip as he flipped through a blue leather journal.

"You…what did you tell Jude?" she asked.

Christian's eyes paused in the centre of the page before they lifted towards her.

"He came to me at the university, asked about her and I told the truth," he said before turning back to the book.

"S-she couldn't have killed Valerie," Audrey replied. "She was with us all night…and Valerie is the only one she's connected to, she never even knew Howell or Little or Foreman or…"

"She buried Foreman and Professor Howell," Christian interrupted. "She must get some sick satisfaction out of it."

"But why remove the…you know," Audrey asked.

Christian dropped his book, tossing it onto the coffee

table before slumping back into his seat with an irritated scowl aimed at his little sister.

"I don't understand the mind of a psychopath, why are you asking me?" he asked.

Audrey's soft face hardened, her hazel eyes narrowing towards him as she pushed herself from the couch, stepping towards him with hot rage bubbling in her chest.

"She's not a psychopath," she spat.

Gripping the arm of the sofa, Christian shot up to meet her, stepping towards her with his towering height difference.

"What would you know about anything anyway?" he asked.

"Quite a bit, despite popular opinion," Audrey replied.

Christian blinked, his features dropping amongst his momentary shock before firming as he bit back.

"You should be grateful she's gone," he said. "She's had such horrid influence on you, although she can't compare to that harlot, Val—"

Audrey's nose scrunched upwards, her eyes radiating with a blinding red as fire of rage rushed through her as she lashed her hand against Christian's face. Her palm stung as she retracted it, her eyes darting between her wrist and Christian's red cheek.

"You just…" he gasped, dropping his palm from his face. "That didn't even hurt."

Closing her fist, Audrey twisted her body as she swung forward. Her teeth sunk into her lip as her knuckles smashed against Christian's chin. Valerie's face flashed across her eyes, the pain sinking into her like winter's frost, tears tickling her lash line as Christian stumbled back with hand on chin and piercing anger burning in his eyes.

"What happened?"

Audrey's eyes darted towards the foyer door, fixating

on Eric as he stepped inside with his eyebrows knitted in the centre of his forehead.

"She punched me!" Christian said, pointing an accusing finger at Audrey.

"I thought you said it didn't hurt," she mumbled.

Christian shot Audrey a scowl before gawking back at Eric as he shrugged his shoulders and loosened his expression into a bitter frown.

"Some brother you are," Christian muttered.

Christian stormed towards Eric, bending his elbow to knock his twin brother in the ribs as he passed. Eric bit his lip as to refuse Christian the satisfaction, keeping his eyes on Audrey as they listened to the deep thumps of Christian's shoes against the staircase. Audrey drew out a long sigh as she clasped her hands together trying to rub away the shadow of violence from her knuckles.

"Where have you been?" she asked.

"Um…I'll show you," Eric sighed.

Audrey followed Eric through the foyer, the coffin still present on the centre island bench. A paint kit and can of brushes sat in the corner of the lid, the wings of the dove peeking out from beneath. The remainder of the lid was coated in a vivid mist of thunder clouds, the sight of which stirred slight disturbance in Audrey's stomach as she found familiar faces twisted into the swirling clouds. Faint figures and gaping expressions gawking back at her, their empty eyes sparkling like stars behind the thick clouds. She clasped her hand over her mouth, turning towards Eric as he gazed over his work.

"You see them too?" she asked.

Eric nodded, sucking on his lips as he glanced back up to Audrey.

"I should've said something," he mumbled.

"You're not the only one…" Audrey sighed. "The letter was for me."

"I know," Eric replied. "I'm so sorry."

Audrey stepped towards him, pressing her face against his chest as he locked his arms around her. She attempted to bury herself into the embrace, hide from the swarming grief filling her chest. Yet she felt out of place in his arms, his hold soft and distant as if she were hugging a stranger and not her beloved big brother.

A LUMP SAT in the base of Audrey's throat as she drifted through the curtains of darkness, following the blank-faced officer down the thin hallway of cells. She skidded to a blunt halt as the officer stopped, turning towards one of the iron-bar doors, inserting a key into the cubic lock before stepping back, pulling the door with him.

"Don't take too long," he said, releasing the door before stepping past Audrey and disappearing back into the corridor.

Audrey sighed gazing through the broken view of the cell before stepping inside, drifting over the figure hiding itself in the corner. Her back faced Audrey as her black hair fell over her neck like a shiny snake, her body as still as a marble statue. The short walls were made of black stone, the floor a smooth grey with only a tiny window wedged at the top of the back wall. Darkness hid in every corner, climbing into the hole in Audrey's chest and pressing down on her shoulders. Audrey bit her lip, pushing a lock of blonde hair behind her ear as she fumbled with the view.

"I-I've never seen you like this," Audrey said.

"This is how they want me," Helena mumbled. "This is how to survive."

"How do you live?" Audrey replied.

"Living, as you call it, brought me right back here," Helena said, drawing her knees into her chest.

"Helena," Audrey said, her voice raspy with frustration as she dropped herself onto the bed.

Her lips hung open, hesitance slapping her as the skin-thick mattress screeched under her weight, the bed jolting before rocking towards a silent stillness. She sighed, a black cloud filling her chest, threatening regret and consequence.

"I can see them too," she said.

Helena's head shifted against the limp pillow, pausing before she tilted her body back towards Audrey, rolling on her back to face her. A cloud of red lay beneath her pale skin, her eyes sparkling with salty tears and her parted lips swollen from smothered tears. The underlying under-standing swarmed Audrey's hesitance, her resolve trembling as she stared back at Helena.

"We're not insane," Audrey said.

Audrey felt a wave of tears itching her eyes, dropping them downwards as Helena reached across her torso to rest her hand on Audrey's, gathering her fingers before giving them a light squeeze. Audrey released a sour breath, rebuilding herself before lifting from the mattress with Helena's hand still gripping her.

"I paid your bail. Let's go," Audrey whispered.

Pulling Helena from the bed, they interlocked arms before guiding each other from the cell. Audrey kept a firm grip on Helena's hand, ignoring the haystack state of her friend's waist-length locks. They met the officer at the door, following him out towards the street. Splashes of fire orange and soap pink coated the late afternoon sky with the occasional black cloud loaming over the blossoming shine. They'd barely begun to step towards Audrey's carriage when the dog called for them.

"Where do you think you're going?"

Helena flinched, her chin dropping to her chest as Jude stormed after them, the double doors of the police station flourishing behind him like wings. Audrey pursed her lips, thick fear growing in her like mould as Jude drew closer. She dug into her hand purse, still linking with Helena as her thin fingers pinched a ward of notes. As Jude parked himself beside them, his hands on his hips and lips parting, Audrey shoved the unknown amount against his chest. His eyes bulged as they darted between her and the notes that he tried to catch between his greedy fingers.

"That should keep you at the table for a few hours," Audrey snapped. "Leave us alone."

Placing her hand on Helena's back, she pushed her towards the carriage, retreating inside as if they were diving into a bomb shelter. Sealing the cabin door shut, she peeked out towards Jude. She scoffed as disgust filled her, watching him chase after the few dropped notes like a fly hovering over rotting fruit.

CHAPTER 19

*H*elena wedged herself into the corner of the carriage, her knees pressing against her chest as she rested her forehead against the window. The jolting of the carriage caused her to involuntarily tap her head against the glass, numbing her further into submissive daze. Another thunderstorm had spread across the sky as they'd exited, leaving the dirt road coated in a thin layer of mud that would soon turn into a dangerous slide of sludge. Helena tuned into the firework rain that bombed the roof of the carriage, ignoring the weight of Audrey's concerned glance from across the cabin. Watching the darkened fields pass by them, Helena's mind jolted back to life as she caught sight of the funeral home, a sudden thought sparking her brain to life like electricity to a machine.

"Stop!" she called.

She waited for the carriage to pull to a partial stop before pushing through the cabin door, skidding in the fresh mud as it sprayed her skirt like blood splatter. Fighting for balance, Helena grasped the graveyard gate, panting before flinging it open.

"Helena!" Audrey called, sticking her head from the carriage.

"I'll meet you back at the house!" Helena replied. "I need to check something, please!"

Helena turned, sprinting through the bullets of rain before bursting into the funeral home. She darted through the rooms before she hunted down a shovel and charged back into the storm as if she were running into a battle-field. With the shovel batting at the raindrops, Helena navigated the graveyard, counting names until she found her man.

*'Matthew Christian Tarter, 1795 – 1855'*

Assaulting the ground with her shovel, Helena began to dig, denting the soggy earth as if she were tearing open a wound. Her body began to heat beneath her soaked dress, the cold rain a partial relief from the exhausting warmth. Her arms filled with hot needles, her back straining like a tense coil as she continued to dig with her throat raw from the rhythm of broken pants.

After a muddled hour of digging Helena exposed the lip of the rested coffin, the varnished wood shining against the flashes of lightning highlighting the shovel dents and scratches to the lip. As Helena heaved out of exhaustion, her eyes racked over the expensive coffin, frowning as she found the nails missing from the lid which was on back-wards. Helena knitted her brows as she lowered herself into the dirt, her skirt absorbing the water as she leaned into the grave, pressing her wet palms against the lid before pushing it aside. Helena yelped as she lost her balance, falling against the slippery coffin with a hard thud. Helena growled, frustration swelling in her chest as she wiped a veil of water from her forehead, freezing as she peeked into the cabin of the coffin. Helena nudged the lid open further, dipping her head down to search the corners, finding it as empty as a butterfly's cacoon.

"Miss!"

Helena flinched at the throaty call, her hand latching to her tightened chest, pressing against her pulsing heart as she gazed off into the darkness. Through the curtains of rain stood a blurred figure approaching her with a heavy limp. Helena's shovel fell into the grass, mild chill rippling down her with the raindrops as she rose to her feet. Her heart burned in her chest as she drew closer, bruising a wet lock of hair from her eye as a flash of lightning illuminated the figure's rotting skin. Foreman moaned at her, rain-water gathering in his open chest falling through him like a drain pipe. Hot tears stung Helena's eyes, locking her arms across her chest, squeezing her forearms as she stuttered over the gunfire rain.

"W-would you like to go now?"

Foreman tilted his head, staggering beneath the weight of the rain before nodding.

Helena extended her arms, raindrops bombing her trembling knuckles as if attempting to bat them down. Helena bit her lip, kicking away her fear as she took a step towards him, locking her elbows to keep her arms unflinching as steel. She clasped his face, gazing into his empty eyes as her fingers travelled across his cheekbones. Foreman recoiled, a high squeak emerging from his blue lips. Helena froze, her breath held captive in her lungs as Foreman squeezed his eyelids shut, lines of black blood dripping from his lash line. Helena bit her lip before sliding her fingers against his lids, closing her eyes as the air evaporated from her lungs.

Wheezing for air, Helena's hands flew back towards her face, smothering her features as a gush of wind caressed her skin. She gasped as a prickly rim flicked her face, dropping her hands to glance upwards. With a flap of his black wings, Foreman's spirit shot up into the air, floating like a black cloud in the sky before dipping back down towards her. Helena held her breath as he zipped by her, skimming the tombstones like a city skyline then disappearing into the forest of raindrops.

🐚

HELENA HUDDLED HOME, dipped in a cold chill, trembling like a frightened puppy by the time she reached the front porch. Her hair hung in wet willow tree veins down her face, her skin as clammy as a frog, and clothes sticking to her like stubborn snake skin. She gripped her shovel with one hand as she reached for the door handle with the other, the rain battering behind her like fireworks. As she stepped inside, she felt another wave of chill, her body flinching as if being slapped by a cold hand. Holding her breath, she glanced to her side to find the cupboard door wedged open with a slice of orange candlelight spilling from the gap. Helena pursed her lips as she listened to the rough rustling inside, identifying the bristled voices of the two men.

"What happened?" Eric asked.

"I don't know," Christian spat.

Helena's frame clinched, her breath clogging in her chest as she caught the biting odour staining the air. Her jaw trembled as the smell of rotting flesh filled her nose, the blank confusion consuming her until she was reduced to a numb statue.

"I'll try another set," Christian sighed.

Helena took a step closer under the prolonged rustling that resumed inside the closet, biting her tongue as one of the wooden panels creaked beneath her shoe, her shoulders hunching as she froze in her place before centring her hearing back towards the closet.

"W-where did you get all of this?" Eric asked with a voice as cold as the night.

"Why curious all of a sudden?" Christian sighed.

"This isn't university-funded research, is it?" Eric said.

"Would you be quiet?" Christian hissed. "You're distracting me."

Helena drew her foot backwards, gripping the shovel with both hands as she slid back towards the front door, her heart pumping thick dread through her veins.

"Helena?"

Thickening dread flushed through her, her blood falling down to her feet as she twisted her neck, gawking up the staircase to find a frowning Audrey. Her frozen heart dropped into her stomach as the closet door opened revealing Christian clad in a lab coat and a pair of leather gloves that glowed a dark red in the dimmed light. They shared a mutual white-shock expression before Helena's eyes wandered over his shoulder and into the closet. Several bright candles lined the sawdust-layered walls, the light bouncing off the bulky metal cabinets that stuck to two of them, followed by a matching operating table resting against the wall opposite the door.

On top of the body sat a white figure painted pale blue with a thick blanket covering his immediate pelvic area. The first wave of shock hit her like a flying bullet, the disbelief spreading through her like a shot of pain before an additional figure stepped into her field of view. Her jaw dropped, her face twisting as a pang of betrayal filled her chest, her lemon-rind glare contrasting Eric's soft gawk.

Helena bent her knees as she lifted the spade of her shovel, swinging it towards Christian with the little strength that remained in her worn muscles. Christian stepped forward, his blank expression turning to that of a growling dog as his hands latched the wooden handle.

"Christian, don't!" Eric shouted.

Helena coughed as Christian lifted his knee, kicking her in the stomach to loosen her grip on the shovel. She stumbled backwards with solid pain flaring in her intestines before the spade of the shovel flashed in front of her eyes, a veil of darkness smothering her as she blended into air around her.

## CHAPTER 20

*H*elena's head pulsed with numbing pain, her eyelids heavy as she huddled in the patch of sunlight that poured through the letter-sized window above her. The attic consisted of the dead space between the second-floor ceiling and the arches of the roof, a collection of spiderwebs and a thick layer of dust that tickled her lungs. Helena chewed on the tight cord that bound her wrist and ankles, her blunt teeth barely denting the strong restraints. Between chomps, she stared at the horizontal trap door that guarded her freedom.

Helena snapped from her fatigued daze as a faint creak lifted from the lower floor, climbing towards her before the trapdoor clicked open. Helena closed her eyes, biting her lip as the door flipped open, tapping against the floor before a heavy creak vibrated across the floor. Helena's eyes snapped open as she swung her legs forward, sending her shoes flying towards her visitor. She yelped as a hard hand gripped her ankles, slamming them down onto the wooden panels. Helena snarled back at Eric as he wrestled with her skirt, his expression flashing between crumbled frustration and soft desperation.

"Stop it! He doesn't know I'm up here," he hissed. "He has a gun, he'll kill us both."

Helena paused, her sharp gaze fixated on Eric who raised his eyebrows as he released his hold on her legs. Helena deepened her frown as he completed his climb, swinging his long limbs out of the hole to lie beside her, propping himself up on the bend of his elbow.

"Where is he?" she asked, sweeping clumps of dust across the floor as she retracted her legs.

"Downstairs with…his project," Eric whispered.

"What the hell is he doing?" she hissed.

Eric sighed, running his hand down his face, his fingers lingering over his closed eyes.

"H-he thinks he can bring our father back," he mumbled. "He thinks if he can…remake the body, the soul will go back inside."

"Using the body parts of his murder victims," Helena replied.

"He told me that he'd stolen parts from the biology department," he said, his voice hitching as he reached to grip her shoulder. "I thought it'd be a childish experiment to help him grieve."

Helena's eyes sharpened as Eric bit his lip, retracting his hand from her before hunching under the weight of her glare.

"He bribed Jude, didn't he?" she said. "You pinned me for five murders."

"I didn't know he killed them," Eric whispered. "I didn't know he could, I didn't even know that he knows how to use a gun or hit a woman over the head with a shovel…I—"

"You let Jude take me away, you knew it wasn't me," she said, her voice deepening as she bit back the tears tickling her lash line. "You're a coward."

Eric's face softened, his dark eyes drifting to the dusty

floorboard as he sucked on his cheeks. Helena deepened her snarl, disgusted by his outward guilt.

"Where's Audrey?" she asked.

"In your bedroom," he mumbled.

"Does she not want to talk to you either?" Helena muttered.

Tucking her hands to her chest, Helena rolled on her back before hauling herself sideways, her back facing Eric. She closed her eyes and hid her face in her forearms, biting her lip as Eric sighed behind her, the panels squeaking as he shifted back towards the shoot, the ladder creaking beneath his weight. The creaking halted, leaving a brief silence before his voice sounded once again.

"Can I ask you something?" he said.

"You can ask, I'm not promising anything in return," she muttered.

"Is there any way to control them or even…get rid of them?" he asked. "I think you know what I'm talking about."

Helena closed her eyes, sighing as she recounted the lecture she'd received form her grandmother the day she was rescued from the asylum, shortening the long explanations into a simple sentence.

"Have you ever seen a cheery ghost?" she asked.

"No," he replied.

"Trauma weighs their souls down to earth, they remain until they're ready to let go," she replied. "Of course, some might need help to do so."

"What if they don't?" Eric asked.

Helena lifted her head from the panels, twisting her neck and poking her shoulder with her chin as she glanced back at Eric.

"Wait until Christian finishes his little experiment and you'll see," she muttered before dropping her head back against the floor.

❧

ROLLING ON HER STOMACH, Helena pushed herself on her knees and elbows, crawling like a stiff caterpillar across the attic, following the makeshift blueprint in her mind until she hovered over the ceiling to her bedroom. Lowering herself back to the floor, she pressed her hot cheek against the prickly wood.

"Audrey?" she hissed. "Audrey?"

"Helena?"

She sighed as she dropped her head against the floor, a smile spreading across her face as relief blossomed inside her chest.

"Are you all right?" Helena asked.

"Yes, he just locked the door and windows," Audrey replied.

"Eric says he has a gun," Helena said, hoping he was once again lying to her.

"Yes, Jude must've given him one..." Audrey said. "What are we going to do?"

"Do you think we could convince him to let us go," Helena replied, toying with the thin idea.

"Father taught him not to respect anyone, even himself," Audrey sighed. "He won't listen to anyone."

Helena bit her lip, tapping her forehead against the floor as she fought back her disappointment. The surrounding walls crawling towards her like impending darkness, the silence sinking into her like a numbing medication.

"God damn!"

Helena jolted as the scream echoed through the house, a shadow cast over her. Twisting towards blocked sunlight, she caught a glimpse of the raven's fleeting wings through the attic window, watching as it trembled mid-air before soaring off into the open horizon. Helena bit her lip as she watched the self-liberated soul drift off in complete freedom that she did not possess.

"Christian calm down, please!" Eric shouted.

Helena gasped, a rush of fear bursting through her as she envisioned the muzzle of a gun aimed at Eric.

"I can help!" she called. "I can help you!"

Helena paused as a wave of silence passed by, her heart pulsing in her chest as she waited for a response.

"What are you doing?" Audrey hissed.

Helena held her breath as a rhythmic military march pierced through the silence, storming up the stairs and towards the attic ladder. Helena rolled over towards the latch door, her heart rolling up into her throat as the door flung open, her body stilling like a frozen deer. The sunlight clung to the bronze casing of the hand gun that shot through the square hole, a mop of black hair following, the owner's sharp black eyes piercing her like a knife. Christian adjusted his stance on the ladder before aiming the pistol towards Helena, drawing the breath form her lungs before muttering.

"What would you know about them?"

"M-my grandmother and a friend of mine studied them," she said, swallowed the fleshy lump in her throat. "I could tell you what's wrong."

"I'm doing just fine," Christian spat.

"Of course, you are," Helena replied.

Helena held her breath as Christian glared at her from behind the gun, his finger stroking the curse of the trigger. Christian sighed like an aggressive bull, his nostrils flaring before he pulled himself through the trap door, crawling towards her with unbreaking dark that she'd only seen in her childhood asylum.

## CHAPTER 21

*H*elena held her breath as her eyes raked over the body of Tarter Senior, pale and bloated like a beached whale with purple stitch wounds running down from the base of his throat to the curve of his belly. The body remained well preserved due to the deep cold that filled the ice room which was well insulated with impenetrable sawdust walls and thick imported snow covering the floors and organ containers.

Christian stood beside her in his lab jacket, his gun still aimed at her as he hovered over the body. Eric stood diagonally beside him, bags growing beneath his eyes as they darted between Helena and Christian.

"H-How long has he been gone?" Helena asked.

"Stop stuttering, it's annoying," Christian snapped.

"Sorry, it's just cold," Helena replied, reaching to grip her forearms.

"Just over six months," Eric said.

Helena bit her lip as she gazed at Eric, her light pondering breaking as he gazed back at her with a stern expression, his eyes jerking down towards the pocket in Christian's lab coat, his hand closing before twisting as if turning a key into a lock. Helena turned back to the body, bending her eyebrows as she pretended to consider Christian's possibilities.

"I-I've never seen a soul return to a body before," she said.

"It has to be possible," Christian replied, sucking his lips with sharp irritation. "If a body is working perfectly, why wouldn't it return?"

Helena glanced over Christian's shoulder as Eric edged closer to his brother, her fingers reaching towards the hidden ring of keys in the lab coat pocket. Her chest began to tightened, her jaw trembling as she muttered.

"You're a little boy playing doctor," she said, "who are you to disturb the dead?"

Christian's face collapsed into a creased frown, fire burning inside his dark eyes as he tilted the gun towards her. Helena's chest numbed as if preparing for the pending bullet. Christian's wildfire glare froze as he flopped forward, a hollow bang filling the room as the bullet shot into the ceiling, a layer of sawdust covering the top of Helena's black hair as Eric shoved Christian over his father's body, the key wedged in his firm grip.

"Go!" Eric screamed.

Helena stumbled from the room, the contrasting temperatures slapping her trembling body, her heart straining her chest as Eric braced himself against the door. Eric bit his lip as Christian began to kick at the door, which shook beneath the force. Eric passed her the key, pressing against the door as she fiddled with the lock, her clammy hands struggling with the metal key. Her stomach dropped as the key refused to slip inside, jarring at the misshapen hole.

"Wrong key," she gasped.

"Let me out, now!" Christian barked.

"Get Audrey!" Eric yelled.

Gripping her skirts, Helena flew up the stairs, gripping the knob of her bedroom door, forcing the key inside before swinging it open. Audrey launched on her and wrapped her arms around her neck as Helena slumped back several steps, placing her hand on the railing to steady herself.

"What's happening?" Audrey asked.

Helena's response lodged in her throat as several splitting bangs shot through the house. A chill sunk into her skin, burning her flesh as she twisted her neck to gaze down the mouth of the staircase.

"Eric," she gasped.

Gripping Audrey's hand, Helena flew down the stairs, stumbling as she reached the final step. Her gut twisted as the scene punched her in the stomach. Eric sat against the door, his once strong legs now limp, his eyes glassy and his arms still open like a pair of wings, pressed backwards against the door in a final attempt to keep it closed.

Audrey screamed as she flung herself towards him, clasping his face as blood began to spill down his back, emerging from beneath his trousers and crawling across the floorboards. Helena clasped her palms over her gaping lips, stumbling over towards them before falling to her knees. Audrey's throaty sobs merged with the background, her face buried into Eric's shoulder.

"I'm sorry, I'm so sorry," he mumbled to her.

Eric turned his head towards Helena, a tear rolling down his cheek as he lifted a hand from the door towards her. Helena took it, squeezing his knuckles as her unsteady breath eased from her trembling lips. Eric groaned as the door shoved him forward, tumbling on Audrey. Helena gripped his shoulders, her throat rolling as her eyes darted between the bullet holes in the door and the blossoming blood staining Eric's back as she dragged him against the wall next to the front door. Audrey clung to the opposite side of him, allowing him to slump against her as his breathing slowed. Christian emerged from the closet, the gun hanging loosely in his grip as he gawked down at his bleeding brother, his lips tilted into a soft frown.

"Look what you've done!" Audrey sobbed. "Is Daddy going to fix this for you? Is Daddy going to take responsibility for this!"

Christian flinched, his mouth hung open as he searched for a reply.

"He needs a hospital," Helena said, looping her head beneath Eric's arm as she attempted to lift him from the floor.

"N-no!" Christian barked, pointing his gun at them.

Helena froze, sinking back to her knees to place her hand on Audrey's back, the other gripping Eric's shoulder as his limp arm strung over hers. She glanced towards him, his eyes half closed and cheek pressed against the top of Audrey's head. Heavy weight pressed down on Helena as if she were stuck at the bottom of a grave with dirt spilling on her body. She removed her hand from Audrey, slipping her forefingers to his still throat, tears spilling from her lash lines as she found no thrumming pulse beneath his cold skin.

"What the hell?" Christian gasped.

Helena glanced past Eric, Audrey and to the front door as it began to creep open, dragging itself across the floor until it revealed a tall woman dressed in a blackened nightgown, smoke oozing from her frog-like skin and her stomach empty like an open wardrobe.

"V-Val?" Audrey whispered.

Valerie glanced down to Audrey, her dark expression fading before turning to Christian, her clouded eyes narrowing towards him as she took a step forward. Christian placed both hands on the handgun, firing twice as she leaped across the room. Helena squealed at each bang, clasping her hand over her mouth as Valerie closed the space between her and Christian, gripping the collar of his shirt as he released a piercing wail.

A loud groan tore through Christian's screams, bursting from the closet and out into the foyer. Helena held her breath, reaching towards Audrey to grip her shoulder as another low moan came from the dark ice room. Several hollow thumps followed then a soft rattling as a figure emerged from the darkness. Naked and grey, it gripped the door frame for balance, the body it inhabited betraying it.

"Father!" Christian screamed, a slight smile spreading across his face.

Valerie recoiled her fingers from Christian's collar, her clouded eyes darting between him and his father. Christian smirked at her like a smug school boy before turning back to Mr Tarter who destroyed his arrogance with a single step. As Tarter slid his foot towards him, his body began to sizzle like meat on a fire, his skin peeling away to reveal the grey flesh beneath. Helena's hand clapped over her mouth as the body slipped off of the soul inside, flames covering the crumbling flesh as it hit the ground with a hard thump. Christian gawked at his creation, the rouge soul staring back at him with piercing red eyes, rotting teeth and hungry aura. Helena held her breath as she gawked at the creature that haunted her, bathed in sunlight instead of the heavy veil of night.

"Father?" Christian said, his confidence trembling with his tone. "It's me, Christian…Junior."

Tarter groaned as he gawked back towards his son, glancing down with disgust at the body beneath him. Helena reached around to grip Audrey's shoulder, tugging with a digging urgency as she jerked her head in the direction of the door. Audrey squeaked as she clung to Eric's corpse, her watered eyes darting between Helena and Valerie.

Tarter stepped towards Christian, drifting over him like a growing storm. Christian remained stubborn in his spot, his body trembling like a leaf in a brisk wind. Helena gave Audrey another rough tug, swallowing as Eric shook in Audrey's tight grip.

"We need to go," Helena whispered.

"We can't leave h—"

Helena's focus darted back to Christian as a piercing scream engulfed the room, filling her core with reactive fear as she watched Christian lifted from the ground, screaming as Tarter's hands clasped his face, smoke steaming from Christian's skin as his legs kicked at the empty air. Helena froze, the image of her uncle replacing Christian before a wet squish tore through Christian's wails. Helena's stomach flipped as blood poured down Christian's cheeks, his father's expression firm as he pressed his thumbs further into his eye sockets. Hypnotised by the scene, Helena gasped as Valerie stepped towards her, her fear vivid despite her rotting features.

"Go!" she screamed.

Helena pulled herself to her feet, tugging at the fabric of Audrey's dress to tear her from Eric. She felt a pulsing sting in her chest as she watched Eric slap the ground like a stuffed doll before locking her arms around Audrey and dragging her towards the door.

Audrey surrendered her fight as they met the fresh air, leading Helena down the porch stairs as sudden silence fell over them like a heavy blanket. Helena felt a kick of relief as her foot reached for the soft dirt at the end of the staircase, her hope snatched away as her hair was pulled at her scalp, dragging her back against the blunt edges of the steps. Her mind stopped as her head hit the stairs, a screen of blur coating her eyes before she focused on the dark figure tugging at her black locks. Valerie clung to his back, covering his eyes as she used her weight to tug him backwards towards the door, his hand still gripping Helena's locks whilst the other swatting at Valerie like a fly.

"No!" Audrey screamed, reaching for her father with rough hands.

Audrey latched on Tarter's arm, her crumbled expression stretching into a painful gape as she retracted her smoking hands. Helena flinched, recalling the day she'd made the same mistake with her uncle, thick helplessness sinking into her like crippling cold.

Tarter's palm pressed against Helena's face, pushing the opposite cheek into the dirt as her skin crumpled beneath his burning grip. Helena screamed, her hands burning as she clawed at his rotting arm. His eyes fixated on her as his fingers brushed her lash line, her iris fuzzing as the heat spread across her eyeball. Biting her lip, her hands flew up towards him, gripping his own rotting features. His crumpled expression sunk into brief confusion before her fingers smothered his sudden fear-struck eyes. His figure burst like a parting cloud, distinguishing like a puff of black smoke. Helena blinked, tears flowing out of the squeezed eyelids as a gush of wind rushed over her with his piercing scream. Three pairs of wings batted by her, frantic *caws* replacing the scream. The two smaller crashed against one another rolling onto the porch whilst the larger landed on the railing of the staircase. Helena lifted her head to gawk back at him, biting her lip as he drew his wings upwards. She flinched as Audrey jumped into view, her face twisted like an old rag as she slapped him with the sole of her shoe. A weak *ah* came from Tarter as he fell to the porch, followed by several caws from Little and Jordan who took off in hurried flight. Audrey climbed the veranda stairs, panting like a taunted bull before approaching Tarter's limp body. She bent her knee before stomping down with her boot, the reactive crunch sending sharp discomfort up Helena's spine.

She watched as Audrey panted, tilting sideways to rest her hip against the railing, cupping her face before crying into her palms. Helena sunk back to the ground, the coolness of the earth drifting up into her body as nauseating numbness swelled in her chest. Her tears stung the hot burn across her face, her vision flickering like unstable candlelight. A mop of blonde hair appeared from the blur, a face emerging within her thin gaze.

"Are you okay?" Audrey asked.

Helena nodded, her head pulsing as Audrey gripped her shoulder, pulling her to lean against the first step of the porch. Helena gasped as she spotted a figure hovering over Audrey, her initial fear fading as she recognised the softened face. Audrey rose to her feet, meeting Valerie's welling stare.

"I'm sorry," Valerie sighed, her voice as thin as ice, "I have to go."

Audrey sniffled, mirrored tears rolling down her hot cheeks as she twisted around to glance down towards Helena.

"H-how do I?" she asked, chopping off her sentence.

"The eyes unlock the soul," Helena said.

Audrey nodded before stepping towards Valerie, cradling her blackened cheeks in her pink hands. Her bottom lip trembled as she huffed a slight sob, her sorrow prompting Helena to dip her eyes down towards the dirt. She flinched as she heard the familiar flap of heavy wings, her eyes rising back up to see a large raven sitting in Audrey's cupped hands. She bit her lip as Valerie spread her wings, waiting for a nod from Audrey before taking off, the wind pushing loose locks of hair away from Audrey's wet face.

CHAPTER 22

With a heavy sigh, Helena sunk onto the single bed, resting the back of her head against the cabin wall as the boat rocked like a baby's cradle. Her clouded eye had reduced her vision to dancing figures and blurred edges as if she were staring at shadows on a cave wall. The black veil she wrapped around her face did little to help, but it hid the wrinkled burns that covered her face like moss up a tree trunk.

Audrey stood across from her at the mirrored bed, placing her suitcase on the mattress before clicking it open, rustling through the few clothes, photographs and trinkets she had packed. Heavy guilt rested in Helena's chest as she watched Audrey file away their forged travel papers, checking the wards of cash she'd hidden in the pockets of her folded clothes. Helena bit her lip, bowing her head as she felt unwelcome in her occupied space.

"I'm going to the deck," she said, reaching for her cane.

"Be careful," Audrey replied.

Helena nodded before lifting herself from the bed, leaning against the wooden cane to play into the guise that she was Audrey's grieving, weak grandmother. Retracing their past steps, Helena moved from the bowels of the ship and onto the front deck, the salty sea air licking at her skin. Over the grumbles of the ocean beneath her, she heard the chatter from the docks below, her heart trembling as she was reminded that they hadn't departed yet. Reaching for the railing, Helena walked a lap around the deck, her veil shielding her from the occasional passenger walking by. She glanced down to the busy docks, catching blurred glimpses of the people passing below: workers carrying crates of supplies, passengers searching their docks, the occasional sailor in uniform.

"Lena!"

Helena froze, her cane knocking against the ship's railing as her eyes darted about the docks until they landed on the owner of the striking voice.

Minerva squinted up at her, her eyebrows arched as she waited to receive confirmation from the woman in the veil. Helena lifted her hand with her palm facing down towards her as fluttering warmth filled her. Minerva mirrored her, smiling back before lowering her hand over her mouth. Helena bit her lip as Minerva turned away, sinking into the black mist of the breathing crowd.

Helena sighed, carrying the heavy weight of the loss in the pit of her stomach as she followed the railing. She began to circle back towards the entrance to the lower deck, squinting past her clouded vision and down the body of the ship to the lapping waves beneath her.

"Madame!"

A sharp chill rippled up Helena's body, her throat clenching as she turned around to see a badge and a small man hiding behind it.

"Police," Jude said, his tone light with uncertainty. "Could you remove your veil please?"

Helena's blood filled with shards of glass, her skin prickling with fear as she glanced down to the crashing waves beneath her and the distant staircase. She swallowed hard, pinching her vocal chords before asking.

"Are you looking for someone, sir?"

"Do you have something to hide?" Jude asked.

She reached up to her wide-rim black hat, unlatching the pin attaching the veil to its brim before drawing it back. Jude's round face drained of colour, his eyes bulging as his lips wedged open as he gawked at her appearance. The scar peaked at the arch of her eyebrow, seeping like a waterfall over her blackened eye, white glaze covering the now highlighted iris, before pouring over the surface of her cheek and trickling down her neck.

"What the hell?" he gasped.

A red glow tore Helena from Jude's gawking expression; a warm figure flicked from behind her dead eye. Her burn prickled as it neared. The blurred outline crystallized a familiar face that soothed her fear.

"Why so quiet, surely you must be proud?" Jude asked.

Helena smiled, her chapped lips piercing her burns as Eric stepped towards Jude, unseen until he placed his cold hand on Jude's shoulder. Jude's face fell, a cloud of fear engulfing him as he glanced to his side, confused until he found Eric standing over him with blackened skin and a dark face on his rotting features.

"W-what?" Jude whimpered, his figure trembling like a strawman in heavy wind.

"Is something the matter?" Helena chirped.

Jude's lips wedged open as he sunk to his knees, hitting the deck with a blunt thump as he held his palms up to face Eric as if waiting to be struck by holy mercy. Eric kept a tight grip on Jude's shoulder, squeezing the soft flesh as he glared down to him with clenched and rotting teeth.

"Do you have that letter?" Helena asked.

"No…"

Helena bit her lip as she felt the bite of disappointment,

taking in a steep breath before lowering her vision back down to him.

"You've seen them and now I promise you, you'll never stop seeing them. They know you're there…" she said. "Do you want to know how to protect yourself?"

Jude nodded, attempting to jerk towards her, whimpering as Eric's hand snagged him, keeping him in place. Helena stepped forward, leaning down so that her face filled his vision, her burns and clouded eyes fixated on him with a dark glare.

"Good luck finding help when everyone thinks you're insane," she whispered. "Go on now."

She glanced up to Eric who sighed before detaching his hand from Jude's shoulder, watching as he stumbled to his feet, whimpering like a puppy before sprinting across the deck, knocking against a group of confused passengers before disappearing down the boarding platform.

Helena sighed, bitterness lingering as she envisioned tossing him overboard or allowing Eric to burn the soul from his eyes. Yet she swallowed it like a large pill before turning back to Eric. He stared at her with his soulless eyes, his face wilted like a flower as his suit hanged from his hungry body. Coldness sunk into her skin as she clasped his face, his soapy eyes boring into her as if there were life still flickering inside. He tilted his face into her left palm, pressing his dead lips against her thumb. Helena bit her lip, a thump swelling in her throat as her fingers travelled to his closed eyes. Helena sniffed as she let her fingers fall forward. She swallowed as she felt weight fall on her left shoulder. She tilted her head towards Eric as he stood on the ball of her shoulder, gazing down at her with a blank expression. Helena gasped as his beak snapped her veil, sending the pin tumbling to the deck as he tugged it free.

"Hey!" Helena hissed.

As she reached for the veil, Eric's wings slapped them away as he took off, soaring overboard with a swift bank. Helena grasped the railing, leaning downward, watching as he found his wings, skimming over the water before lifting up into the sky. As the ocean wind licked her burns, she watched with a strained heart as he faded into the thick smoke that layered the London horizon.

"There you are!"

Helena smiled as Audrey crossed the deck towards her, removing her hat before her friend met her at the railing. A crowd began to gather as the ship started to separate from the dock, drifting like a heavy leaf through a soft stream in contrast to its bulking size.

"Where's your veil?" Audrey asked.

"I don't need it," Helena said, looping her arm around Audrey's.

Audrey smiled placing her hand on Helena's bicep as her eyes glanced back towards the fading land.

## ACKNOWLEDGMENTS

Thank you to Nadia Gerassimenko, the best editor ever, for your guidance, friendship, compassion and for being one of the few who believed in my writing.

Thank you to Leza Cantoral (and all the other beautiful humans at CLASH Books) for your kindness and encouragement, and for giving me the opportunity to publish this novella.

Thank you to my dear friend Loretta for the many cups of peppermint tea and your lessons in how to give less fucks.

Thank you to Celia Schouteden, for being a wonderful friend, editor and supporter.

Thank you to the wonderful Magda Knight, the first to publish my work online, and to the amazing Tianna G. Hansen, for your kind words and support.

# ABOUT THE AUTHOR

Claire L. Smith is an Australian writer and filmmaker whose various short stories and poetry are featured in publications such as Dark Marrow, Peculiars Magazine, The Horror Tree, Death and The Maiden, Moonchild Magazine and more. She currently oversees fiction, creative nonfiction and poetry at mental-health awareness publication, Peculiars Magazine.

Helena is her debut novella.

Her website is www.clairelsmith.com and her Twitter/Instagram is @clairelsmxth

ALSO BY CLASH BOOKS

**TRAGEDY QUEENS: STORIES INSPIRED BY LANA DEL REY & SYLVIA PLATH**
Edited by Leza Cantoral

**GIRL LIKE A BOMB**
Autumn Christian

**CENOTE CITY**
Monique Quintana

**HEXIS**
Charlene Elsby

**I'M FROM NOWHERE**
Lindsay Lerman

**BURIALS**
Jessica Drake-Thomas

**NO NAME ATKINS**
Jerrod Schwarz

**HORROR FILM POEMS**
Poetry by Christoph Paul & Art by Joel Amat Güell

**NIGHTMARES IN ECSTASY**
Brendan Vidito

WE PUT THE LIT IN LITERARY

CLASHBOOKS.COM

FOLLOW US

TWITTER

IG

FB

@clashbooks